Robert was determined to kiss someone. Even if it was Jenny.

He heard her first soft, shocked breath as he drew her to him. He was close enough to feel her second indignant breath as he bent his head.

The camera flashed. The talking stopped.

Robert was triumphant. His big moment was recorded. He could end the kiss. But he didn't. Something was happening.

The kiss blossomed. Jenny tasted of home. The minute Robert felt her lips tremble beneath his, he was lost. He didn't want the kiss to end. He felt like he had caught a fragile thread of something precious he didn't even understand....

Books by Janet Tronstad

Love Inspired

An Angel for Dry Creek #81
A Gentleman for Dry Creek #110
A Bride for Dry Creek #138
A Rich Man for Dry Creek #176

*Dry Creek

JANET TRONSTAD

grew up on a small farm in central Montana. One of her favorite things to do was to visit her grandfather's bookshelves, where he had a large collection of Zane Grey novels. She's always loved a good story.

Today, Janet lives in Pasadena, California, where she works in the research department of a medical organization. In addition to writing novels, she researches and writes nonfiction magazine articles.

A Rich Man for Dry Creek

Janet Tronstad

Published by Steeple Hill Books™

STEEPLE HILL BOOKS

Steeple
Hill™

ISBN 0-373-87183-X

A RICH MAN FOR DRY CREEK

Copyright © 2002 by Janet Tronstad

This edition published by arrangement with Steeple Hill Books.

Visit us at www.steeplehill.com

Printed in U.S.A.

It is easier for a camel
to go through the eye of a needle
than for a rich man to enter into the kingdom of God.
—*Mark* 10:25

This book is dedicated with love to my nieces

Julie Miller
Sara Enger
Marcy Enger MacDonald
LaRae Tronstad
Starla Tronstad

Chapter One

❦

"**J**ust because he's rich doesn't mean he's crazy." Jenny Black pressed the cell phone to one ear and stood on her tiptoes to look at another dusty shelf in the old pantry. Her sister should stop worrying about Robert Buckwalter's sanity.

She should worry about Jenny's instead.

Jenny was the one who was crazy.

What was she thinking? Trying to cater a black-tie dinner in a place like Dry Creek, Montana. Right now Jenny was in the pantry of the town's small café and she was desperately looking for paprika.

Jenny had made a big mistake. She should never have promised hors d'oeuvres to go with the lobsters she was serving tonight.

The ranching community of Dry Creek, tucked up close to the Big Sheep Mountains in southern Montana, was absolutely delightful. But any sane chef would have insisted the menu be switched to chili dogs and corn chips the minute she discovered the only store in town sold ten kinds of cattle feed and not one single thing for a human to eat.

Jenny had not been able to buy any of her last-minute supplies.

She'd turned for help to the couple who ran the café but they were only set up to serve hamburgers, biscuits and spaghetti. They had sugar packets, squeeze bottles of honey and those plastic packets filled with ketchup. There was not one obvious hors d'oeuvre in sight.

She was doomed.

Jenny heard an impatient grunt on the other end of the phone.

"Sorry, but if you ask me, Mr. Buckwalter is so sane he's almost comatose." Jenny had tried earlier to make conversation with the man. No luck. "Stuffed-shirt kind of sane. Think Dad."

"But Dad's fifty years old!"

"Well, Robert Buckwalter acts like he's a hundred." Jenny still felt a twinge of pique. The whole world knew that her employer's son, Robert Buckwalter, was a ladies' man. He was supposed to flirt with all women.

Jenny had expected to dodge a compliment or two on the flight over. But the man had sat in the pilot's seat next to her the whole flight and not said anything at all once he'd made sure she'd fastened her seat belt. For which, she told herself firmly, she should be grateful. And she should be fair to the man. "Of course he's most helpful—especially when he's got an apron around his waist."

"He's got an apron on!"

"Well, he's helping me with the hors d'oeuvres. We've got a hundred people coming for dinner—Maine lobsters—and I've had to improvise with the hors d'oeuvres."

Improvise was putting it lightly, Jenny thought. Try egg salad on toast—which wouldn't be so bad if she could at least find something to sprinkle on top of it.

"Robert Buckwalter the Third is cooking for you—and he has an apron on!" Jenny's sister couldn't let go of that thought.

"Well, it's only some carrot stubs. It's not like he's whipping up a soufflé or anything complicated."

"But he doesn't even grill. It says that in his bio. My word, do you know how much money the man has?"

The question was obviously rhetorical and Jenny didn't answer.

She had enough to do pushing aside spice tins hoping for some paprika.

The Dry Creek café had been abandoned years ago and left empty until a couple of teenagers had reopened it this past December on the night of the town's first annual Christmas pageant. The original owners must have decided some supplies weren't worth hauling out of Dry Creek because stray cans and tins had been left behind to sit quietly, collecting dust, for all those years.

"A little kitchen work never hurt anyone," Jenny said. You'd think she was exploiting children or something. The idle rich were not a protected species.

"You're not bossing him around, are you? Please tell me you're not bossing him around."

"He volunteered!"

"Good, because he *is* Robert Buckwalter the Third."

"Give me some credit. I know how it is with the rich."

Jenny didn't have to remind her sister that, when they were kids, it was the fancy cars of the rich people who had always come to the suburban area near them to drop off their unwanted pets.

Apparently her sister not only remembered the cars, she also remembered that Jenny had been the one to shake her fist at the drivers as they sped away. "Look, Jenny, it's important that you're nice—you know, give him a chance to like you."

"Me? Why?"

"Well, maybe he'll talk to you. Tell you things. I could use some help here. I think the only reason

I got my job is because you are working for the Buckwalters and my boss thought you'd be able to tell me stuff for the paper. Like this list of one hundred bachelors we're working on. Buckwalter's at the top, so far, and I'm counting on you to tell me about him.''

Jenny sighed. ''You shouldn't have taken the job then. It's not right. Besides, I don't have anything to tell. I hardly know the man.''

''He answered your phone.''

''This isn't my phone. It's the Buckwalter business phone. It's supposed to be for business calls only. I'm surprised the main office gave you the number.''

A dim lightbulb hung down from the ceiling and Jenny had to squint to see the top shelf where restaurant-size spice containers were shoved behind several cans of what must be lard even though the labels were so faded they were hard to identify.

''Well, I may have said something about business—''

''What business?''

''Well, this *is* a business question. Something's wrong. I've been working it out. The man is either crazy or secretly married. He's always been in the tabloids. I know—I almost crashed my computer doing a word search on him. Dozens of pieces. This party. That woman. The next party. The next woman. And then—bingo—it all stops. Our top sources couldn't even get the man to return a phone call! And they're his friends.''

"His friends spy on him?"

"Well, you know how it is with the rich. They all do that. But that's not the point. The point is that no one's seen him. There's been nothing for the last five months.'' Jenny's sister paused and then continued. "I'm hoping you know why. My editor is getting nervous. We need to decide if we're going to make Robert Buckwalter number one on our bachelor list. Do you know what that means to be number one? Men would kill for that spot. You can make a million just endorsing stuff—shaving cream, shoes, clothes. It's a gold mine. But we certainly don't want to give the title to Buckwalter if he's wacko or married. We'd look like fools who didn't even know what was going on in the world.'' She sighed. "Do you really think he could be married?"

"I doubt it—surely, he'd tell his friends if he got married.''

"Not if she was unsuitable.''

Jenny paused. She remembered she wasn't the only one to protest those rich cars when they were kids. Her sister was there, too. "You don't need to worry. It's not like he married a kitten who grew up to be too much trouble. Even the rich don't treat their wives that way.'' Well, usually not, she added silently. "Besides, I thought that anything goes with the rich these days—look at that blond singer. Underwear in public. Pierced tongues. There's not much left to be unsuitable.''

''She could be poor.''

Jenny's lips tightened. ''If that bothers him, then he shouldn't have married her in the first place.''

''Is he wearing a wedding ring?'' her sister asked.

''I don't think so.''

''Don't you know? Goodness, Jenny, don't you even look anymore? Talk about him being comatose. You're turning positively ancient yourself.''

''I am not! Twenty-nine is young.''

''If you don't look at the ring finger, believe me, you're old.''

''Well, I'm pretty sure he didn't have a ring. I remember giving him the knife, and I always check for rings—some people like to take them off so they don't get wet.''

''You're getting him wet! Robert Buckwalter the Third.''

''Even rich people need their vegetables washed.''

Her sister was silent for a minute before continuing. ''Wait a minute. Are you sure this is Robert Buckwalter the Third? Maybe there's been some kind of a mix-up. A kidnapping or something. This just doesn't sound right—vegetables and aprons. He doesn't even know how to make coffee. It says that, right in his bio.''

Jenny smiled. "So far, he hasn't made coffee, and his mother seems to believe it's him."

"Well, what does she say about him being gone all that time? Is she worried he's married?"

"She hasn't said a thing. And I don't know why you think he's married. Just because he kept to himself for a while, doesn't necessarily mean he's been to the altar. Maybe he's just tired," Jenny said as she spied the can of paprika and reached for it. "Five months isn't so long to rest if he keeps a social schedule like the one you've talked about— it sounds grueling."

"I never thought of that." Her sister was horrified. "Maybe he's worse than tired—maybe he's sick."

"Oh, I doubt he's sick," Jenny said as her hand wrapped around the can of paprika. She'd have to taste it to see if it was still good. "But I wouldn't know for sure. I just work for him—well, really for his mother. I'm the chef—I'm in charge of parties like this one tonight. That's it. It's not like I know the man personally."

"You must know something about him."

"I know what he eats." Jenny looked through the pantry door into the kitchen at the man in question. "Heavy into vegetables and meats—beef, lamb, duck—he likes them all." That certainly didn't sound like a man who was sick.

She suddenly remembered that she did know

more about Robert Buckwalter than what he ate. But her sister wasn't interested in the fact that some man had an odd aversion to her hair net, which was a perfectly fine hair net and required for food handling—even if it did make her look like a monk.

"There's got to be more. Think. This is important."

Jenny wiped the dust off the can of paprika. She'd been more mother than older sister to her three siblings and it seemed like one or the other of them always had something important that needed her help even though they were all over eighteen by now and should be adults.

She stood in the open doorway and studied the tall man that was causing her sister so much worry.

The light in the kitchen came from two bare bulbs hanging directly over the long counter that divided the square room. The kitchen walls were white. The sink and refrigerator were both forty years old and chipped. It was a humble kitchen.

Now that her sister mentioned it, Jenny wondered why the man had volunteered to help. She certainly hadn't expected it of him. No one else had, either. Even his mother had looked up in pleased surprise when he'd demanded a knife and a bunch of carrots.

Jenny studied his profile, looking for answers.

At first glance, the man was the classic movie star ideal. The kind of actor that always wore the white hat. The aristocratic nose was perfectly balanced.

The glossy black hair was combed stylishly in place. The cheekbones closely barbered. He looked like a luxury car ad. Definitely your playboy kind of a guy.

But as she looked closer, Jenny noticed some fraying. He had a bruise on the side of his forehead. It was faint, but it was there. His hair was nicely combed, but there was something off center and a little ragged about the cut. And his tan was uneven, like he might have been wearing a cap—not a designer cap with the bill turned to the back like a baseball player, but an old-fashioned cap like a farmer would wear.

My word, Jenny thought, my sister might be on to something.

Jenny didn't think the man was sick—his cheeks looked too healthy—but Robert Buckwalter certainly had the neglected air of someone who was letting himself go to seed.

He might just be married at that.

That would certainly explain the plane trip over here. The man had insisted—not offered, but flat-out insisted—on personally flying Jenny and the lobsters from Seattle to Dry Creek in his fancy plane.

Jenny had been surprised he was going to Montana. He had just arrived at his mother's house in Seattle from some trip that he wouldn't explain. He looked tired and was limping. The housekeeper had his suite of rooms made up and ordered the customary orchids for his bedside table. Then the housekeeper put in the standing order for extra staff to handle the usual parties.

Robert Buckwalter hadn't been home for twenty minutes before he canceled the orders. The housekeeper said he walked into his rooms and looked around as though he didn't know where he was or why he was there.

Then he announced he was going to fly to Dry Creek to talk to his mother. He must have had something urgent to tell her—like maybe that he had a wife. Jenny wondered how the older woman would take the news of a strange daughter-in-law.

Mrs. Buckwalter was financing a winter camp for some teenagers from Seattle and the woman was staying in Dry Creek to be sure that all went well. It was a fine, giving gesture and Jenny respected the older woman for it.

But Jenny knew her sister wasn't interested in Mrs. Buckwalter. There must be something useful about the man in question that she could share with her sister.

"Even if he's not sick, I think he might have corns."

"What?"

"You know—corns on his feet. And bad. I remember his mother commenting on some bill he'd run up for corn pads. Hundreds of dollars."

Her sister grunted. "The man's an Adonis. He can have a gazillion corns on his feet and who cares?

No one's looking at his feet. Have you even stopped your cooking long enough to look at the man?''

"Well, of course, I have."

"And?"

"He's neat, well dressed, clean—"

"Clean!"

"Well, he is—more than most."

"I've got a news flash for you! He's a whole lot more than clean. He's hot. Drop-dead gorgeous. And if you haven't noticed that I'm really worried about you. Might even talk to Mom about it. She always says you're too picky—wait until she finds out you're even picky with him. Robert Buckwalter—"

"I know."

"—the Third."

A timer went off in the kitchen.

"Look, I've got to go," Jenny said in relief. "I've got egg puffs that need to come out of the oven."

The café kitchen was noisy. A group of teenage girls, wearing prom dresses from the fifties, stood at a table in the corner laughing and folding pink paper napkins into the shape of swans. A dozen of the boys stood beside Robert Buckwalter, following his moves as they cut chunks of carrot into the closest thing they could get to a flower. The carrot nubs were more tulips than roses, but they had a charm all their own.

Jenny had forgotten the boys were from a Seattle street gang until she saw their ease with knives.

Some of those boys could have done credible surgery on something larger and more alive than a hunk of carrot.

Jenny was thankful for people like Sylvia Bannister who ran a center for gang kids in Seattle, and for Garth Elkton who had welcomed the kids to his ranch for a winter camp program. Jenny had seen how peaceful the Big Sheep Mountains looked in the snow. Low mountains skirted by gentle foothills. This little ranching community was a perfect haven for gang kids.

Sylvia and Garth were giving those kids a second chance. Mrs. Buckwalter was funding the winter camp and providing the lobsters tonight, both as a thanks to the community of Dry Creek, especially to the minister who had recently gotten married, and as a reward to the teenagers from Seattle for putting down their knives and learning to dance.

Sylvia and Garth were the kind of people that deserved to be number one on some New York tabloid list, not some hotshot rich man like Robert Buckwalter who spent half his life in Europe attending art shows, Jenny told herself. He didn't even organize the shows; he just sat there and gave away money.

Jenny felt a twinge of annoyance. An able-bodied man like Robert Buckwalter should be more useful in life. Giving away money hardly qualified as a job—not when he had so much of it. She doubted he even wrote the checks himself.

"I ruined one of the mushrooms," a girl wailed from the sink. "Totally ruined it. The stem didn't come out right and—"

"Not a problem. We just cut it up and put it with the stuffing." Jenny walked to the refrigerator to get out the herbed bread mixture that went in the few mushroom caps they'd found in the café's refrigerator bin. "Nothing goes to waste in a good kitchen. There's always some other place for it. If nothing else, there's soup. 'Waste not, want not' my mother always used to say. And remember, aprons everyone."

The kids groaned.

Robert Buckwalter grunted. He wondered if he was crazy. He shouldn't be annoyed with the ever-resourceful Jenny. He should be grateful to her. After all, he'd hired her because of her apparent good cheer and her complete indifference to him.

During her job interview, she'd asked no personal questions about him—no sly inquiries about how often he'd be present for dinner at his mother's home in Seattle, or whether as the family chef, she'd be required to fly to the flat he must have in London or maybe the villa he had in Venice or the chalet he had in the Alps…and surely he must have at least one of those, didn't he? Or maybe he just traveled around in the plane he had, the one especially designed with all the gadgets, the one she'd read about in the papers, the one they called the ultimate "rich man's" toy?

The questions would come. They always did.

Except with Jenny.

But then, maybe she'd just been more clever than most.

"Finished with the phone?" Robert asked politely. He hadn't been fooled for a minute by the woman who had called claiming she needed to speak to Jenny urgently about some pudding order. Pudding, my foot. The woman was no salesperson.

Why else would Jenny take the call and disappear into that hole of a pantry where no one could hear her conversation?

Not even bats would go into that pantry if they didn't have to. Jenny had literally needed to pry the door open earlier with a crowbar. The wood was half-rotted and the wind blew in through the knotholes.

No, it wasn't a place where anyone would go for a cozy phone conversation with a pudding salesperson.

Robert Buckwalter swore he could spot a reporter a mile off and he had a bad feeling about that call.

Maybe his time was up.

Robert knew how to keep a low profile with the press but he was off his game. He'd gone completely rustic. On the flight over here, he'd looked at all the extra knobs on his plane's instrument panel and wondered what he'd ever need with all the unnecessary attachments he'd asked the manufacturer to add. He couldn't even remember why he'd wanted a cup-size blender added on the passenger side.

He hardly knew himself anymore. It came from spending a whole five months as someone else.

Jenny carefully laid the phone back down on the counter where it had been when the last call arrived and then picked it up again to wipe off the dust that had followed her out of the pantry.

Robert watched her as he untied the apron strings from around himself and put the damp apron on the nearby counter. "Hope there was no problem."

She looked up at him in alarm. "What?"

"About the pudding," Robert elaborated grimly. She looked confused and guilty as sin. "I hope there was no problem with the order."

"No, no, everything's fine." Jenny blushed.

Robert wondered what the tabloids were paying these days. "Good. I'm glad to hear that. Wouldn't want anything to go wrong with...things."

Jenny stiffened. "I run an efficient kitchen. Everything will be fine."

"Of course."

"I'll admit we are a little behind schedule, but your mother assured me that people will be late arriving because of the cold weather. And everything's set up in the barn. Tables, chairs—the works. The kids even decorated.''

Jenny hadn't worried when she was in Seattle and Mrs. Buckwalter had called to ask her to come cater this event. The older woman had said the party was to be held in The Barn. She'd announced the fact with such flourish that Jenny assumed it was some bohemian restaurant with theme.

Jenny was startled when they drove into Dry Creek and she saw that The Barn really was a barn, complete with hayloft and straw. Then she looked around at the few buildings in town and realized there probably wasn't an industrial oven in any one of them.

That's when she first knew she was in trouble. Not that it would do to admit it to her employer's son.

''We'll have the platters ready just as soon as those puffs cool. And the water's heating for the lobsters. A half hour and dinner will be served.''

Robert nodded as he picked up the cell phone she had laid back on the kitchen counter. He slipped it into his pocket. His phone had a redial feature built into it. Maybe he could call the reporter and stop the story.

Robert put on his wool overcoat and stepped outside. Snow covered patches on the ground and the frigid air made his breath catch. He'd been in cold weather before at ski resorts, but the cold in rural Montana bit harder.

The back door to the kitchen led to a dirt path that was lined with garbage cans. Fortunately, the temperature was so cold the garbage wasn't rotting. Not that Robert minded the smells of garbage anymore.

Robert wondered if he'd ever be the same again. He hadn't intended to spend five months as someone else. It had started as the adventure of a bored rich man. He knew that. There was something supremely arrogant about shedding his identity like it was last year's fashion.

But he had done it and wasn't the least bit sorry.

He'd flown down to the Tucson airport last October. From there he'd headed on foot toward a little town on the Arizona/New Mexico border. He'd left his suit with his plane in a locked area of the airport. He also left his black diamond watch and his laptop computer.

He walked away wearing an old pair of denim jeans and a flannel shirt. The only thing expensive about his clothes had been his tennis shoes. He had no car. No cell phone. A dozen twenty-dollar bills, but no credit cards.

He still remembered how good it felt.

That day he left behind Robert Buckwalter III and became simply Bob. He rolled the name around on his lips again. Bob. He liked the sound of it. It was friendly in a way Robert could never be.

Robert had intended to spend a week alone in the desert at some flea-bitten motel along the highway so that he could return to his parties with more enthusiasm. He certainly didn't intend to be stuck as Bob. He was merely cleansing his palate, not giving up the rich life he enjoyed.

But that first day he discovered Bob was the kind of guy people talked to. Robert was amazed. He'd never realized until then that people didn't talk to him; they mostly just told amusing stories and agreed with everything he said.

They were, he concluded in astonishment, handling him. How could he have not noticed?

He didn't have friends, he realized. He had groupies.

An old man in a beat-up truck had given Robert a ride south out of Tucson and invited him to share supper. Supper had been spicy beans and warm rice with a toaster pastry for dessert. The plate he used had been an old pie tin and the glass had been a jelly jar. The fork he ate with had a tine missing.

But the whole meal had been given in kindness and it tasted very good. When it was finished, the old man offered him a job earning twenty-five dollars a day chopping wood for his winter's supply.

Robert had been about to refuse. He had enough money in his pocket for meals and a cheap hotel.

He didn't need a charity job. But something in the man's eyes tipped him off and instead he looked at the woodpile and saw it was empty except for a few scrub branches.

The old man couldn't chop anymore. He needed help. Robert offered to chop some wood to repay the man for supper.

One meal led to the next and the woodpile grew. Robert's days found a rhythm. He slept in a camper shell by one of the old sheds on the man's property. The nights were a deep quiet and he slept more peacefully than he ever remembered.

Each morning he woke up to the disgruntled crowing of a red rooster he'd nicknamed Charlie. Charlie had no trouble making his opinions known; he had never learned to bow down to the opinions of the rich. He didn't even respect the opinions of nature. He seemed to be particularly unhappy with the sun each morning.

Robert didn't want to chop wood in the chill of the early morning—and especially not with Charlie strutting around. Robert had never seen anything as cranky as that red bird in the morning. You'd think the morning had come up as a personal insult to the rooster. At least Charlie took it that way.

So, instead of listening to Charlie, Robert would jog down the hard-packed dirt road for several miles. He aimed himself in the general direction of the mountains even though they were so far away he'd never get there by running. But he liked to look at them anyway.

His morning run took him past two run-down houses with an astonishing assortment of children spilling out of each. Toddlers. Teens. Boys. Girls. One morning some of the children started to follow him on his run. Before the end of the week, a dozen kids were trailing after him and he was carrying the smallest in a backpack he made from a blanket.

It took a full week for them all to tell him their names.

It was the second week before Robert noticed most of them were running in thin sandals and slippers.

Robert almost scolded them for not dressing right for running, when he realized they were wearing the only shoes they had. The next morning he brought some old newspaper with him and had the kids each make a drawing of their right foot for him.

Later that day he hitchhiked to the nearest post office and sent an overnight package to his secretary ordering fourteen pairs of designer tennis shoes just like his.

The shoes arrived on a Monday.

It was Thursday before Robert saw the children were all limping and he realized he had forgotten socks. How blind could he be? He'd realized then just how removed he'd always been from the needs of others.

He gave money, but it was other people on his staff who actually worried about the arrangements. He, himself, paid very little attention to the needs of others. His contribution was reduced to a dollar sign. It was a picture of himself that he didn't particularly like.

Unfortunately, others still had a fascination with his wealth and the tabloids fed their interest.

Too bad he wasn't still living in the camper shell with Charlie, Robert thought. Charlie might like being in the tabloids.

Robert had discovered he didn't like being in tabloids. In fact, he could honestly say he hated it more than Charlie hated the morning.

Robert removed the phone from his pocket and pushed the redial button. He wondered how much it would cost to kill the story.

Not that it mattered. Whatever it was, he already knew he'd pay it.

Chapter Two

Robert Buckwalter didn't ordinarily notice the stars in the sky. But, standing still, holding the cell phone in his right hand, he looked up and blinked. Montana had a blackness to the nights that calmed him. He'd spent too much time in cities with all their noise and lights.

All of the commotion stopped a man from thinking.

And he needed to think his way out of this situation. Money wasn't enough this time.

Jenny's sister had crumbled when she realized who was on the other end of the phone. Robert had not even needed to be stern. The young woman confessed why she'd called her sister and apologized for asking questions.

She was contrite. She was abashed.

She was useless.

Robert had groaned inside when he found out why the young woman had called. He had dreaded the bachelor list even before his five months in Arizona. What sane man wouldn't?

The bachelor list winners might as well enroll in a circus freak show. No one left them an ounce of privacy. Or dignity. Last year he'd been number seventeen. Some tabloid had printed the sizes of all one hundred men's underwear. Ten different women had actually sent him silk boxers with their names screened on them.

And the letters! He had over a hundred letters from strange women asking him to marry them.

Just imagine if he was in the number one spot. They might as well shoot him now before his mailman filed for workman's compensation because of the backache from delivering those letters—a fair number of which would come with a string-tied package. Somehow the packages with string on them always included baked goods. Chocolate-chip cookies. Plum bread. One enterprising woman had shipped a pot roast in a gallon-size zipper bag because some tabloid story had mentioned he liked beef.

And the underwear givers and the cookie bakers were not even the worst of the lot. The more aggressive called on the telephone and demanded to talk to him. They wouldn't take no for an answer.

They knew how to dodge every polite refusal. His secretary was likely to quit this time around.

Maybe he should hire Charlie to take those calls.

Robert, himself, wasn't interested in a wife that came from a list.

It was old-fashioned, but Robert knew if he ever did marry it would be a real marriage. One that lasted a lifetime. Not one based on lists or money. Odd as it sounded, he'd realized in his five months away that he wanted a wife who would want a simple home with him. Without servants and expensive antiques. Someone who would want him to mow the lawn and take out the trash. Someone who would talk to him and not just quietly pretend to find whatever he was talking about fascinating enough for both of them.

A woman like that probably didn't even read the tabloids. She certainly wouldn't mail him a pot roast or a pair of boxers if she didn't know him.

No, if Robert ever wanted to live a normal Bob-like life, he needed to start it now. He needed to get off the list.

The trouble was he didn't trust the young woman he'd spoken with to simply tell her editors that Robert Buckwalter thanked them very much for thinking of him, but could they please think of someone else for their bachelor list.

Fortunately, Robert knew one thing and that was the celebrity world. He'd been forced to learn how it worked. He knew stories were killed every day and that lists could go up in smoke with the wrong move.

As Robert saw it, he had one chance to change things and that was to make himself very unpopular. He needed to do something that would alienate women everywhere. He'd asked the woman and she'd confessed that the list was to be released on February 29. Leap Year's Day. Women's choice. It was already February 20. He needed to act fast.

First, a victim must be found. He found that nothing set off women better than mistreatment of one of their own. And Jenny, the chef, must know about the action so she could tell her sister who would then tell her employers. That should get his name thrown off the list and into the trash.

Robert felt better already. All he had to do was be obnoxious. His feet were still sore, but he was sure he could be sufficiently unpleasant to raise some eyebrows.

Confident that his troubles would soon be over, Robert slipped the cell phone back into the pocket of his overcoat and started to whistle.

He was almost cheerful when he stepped back into the kitchen. It wouldn't be too hard. Before long his reputation would be back where it belonged—in tatters.

All he needed to do was find a woman to persecute.

Robert stepped into the kitchen to find it empty of everything except steam. He walked over to the stove and looked into one of the big lobster pots. It was empty, as well.

Good, he thought to himself in satisfaction, the party was starting. An audience would be helpful for what he needed to do.

The dining room of the café had been turned into a girl's dressing room and Robert walked quickly through the haze of perfume. Makeup was scattered over the table closest to the door and several pairs of high heels were lined up along the right wall.

Robert stopped in front of the mirror taped to the inside of the door and ran a comb through his own hair. He brushed a few snowflakes off the shoulders of his overcoat. The overcoat was black. His suit underneath was black. Each cost more than most men made in a month.

Robert nodded at his reflection with satisfaction; he looked good. Every man should look good on his way to his own public scandal.

The first bite of the cold when he stepped out the front door made him step even faster. The café was just down the gravel road from the barn where the party was to be held and the space between was full of old cars and trucks. This part of Montana certainly wasn't prosperous, he thought as he spied the old cattle truck that was parked next to the bus his mother had rented to haul all the teenagers around.

He nodded to an old man who was weaving between the cars with a bottle of beer in his hand.

"Coming to the party?" Robert looked closer at the man.

"Ain't been invited." The man's beaten face looked anxious in the moonlight.

"Everyone's invited," Robert said firmly. The old man looked like he could use a good meal that didn't slide down from the neck of a brown bottle. "What's your name?"

The old man looked startled. Robert didn't blame him. He was startled himself. Since when had he cared about the names of poor old men?

"Gossett."

"Well, Mr. Gossett, I hope you'll come have some dinner with us."

"I ain't dressed for it."

The man was wearing a beige cardigan sweater covered with what looked like cat hair and a thermal undershirt that had a yellow ring around the band. His neck was scrawny and his eyes were bloodshot. His denim jeans had grease stains on the knees. Only the man's boots looked new.

"This will set you up," Robert said as he took off his overcoat and offered it to the old man. "Put that on and you'll be right in fashion."

Warm, too, Robert thought to himself.

The man's startled look turned to alarm. "You with the Feds?"

"The who?"

"The FBI. They don't think I seen them. But they're here. Sneaking around in the dark. Watching me."

"They're not watching you," Robert said gently as he offered the coat again. "I've heard there's been some cattle rustling reported. Interstate stuff. It's been going on for some time and they can't get a handle on it. That's why they're here. It's just the cattle. It's nothing for you to worry about."

Robert knew the FBI was in Dry Creek. One of their agents had questioned Jenny and himself when they'd landed with the lobsters out near Garth Elkton's ranch the other night.

"You know who they think done it?" the man asked, leaning so close that Robert got a strong whiff of alcohol. "The rustling?"

"No, I don't think they know yet." Robert wondered if he should insist the man come into the warmth of the barn. With the amount of alcohol the man was drinking, it was dangerous for him to be out in the freezing temperatures. "You're sure you don't want to borrow the coat? You'd be welcome to eat with us."

The man carefully set his bottle of beer on the hood of an old car before reaching out toward the coat. "I might just get me a little bit of something. It sure smells good."

The two men walked inside the barn together.

The old man headed toward the table set up with appetizers. Robert resisted the urge to go over and visit his carrot flowers. Instead he looked around for the woman he needed.

There was a sea of taffeta and silk. Young teenage girls with heavy lipstick and strappy high heels. Farm wives with sweaters over their simple long dresses. A couple of women who looked unattached.

And, of course, the chef.

If he had his choice, Robert would persecute the chef. If for no other reason than to rattle her calm and make her take off that hair net of hers. It was a party. She could loosen up. But the only thing he could think to do was to kiss her, and that certainly wasn't outrageous. The media would just think he'd taken another in a long line of girlfriends. They'd yawn in his face.

No, he needed something shocking.

He looked over the teenagers and settled on the youngest one. His kissing her would raise the hackles of the tabloid world. She looked to be little more than a child, no more than twelve. Women all across the country would raise their handbags in unison to clip him a good one and he'd deserve it.

Robert went over to the buffet table. He'd look less threatening if he had one of those plastic cups in his hand. After all, he wanted to kiss the girl, not have her pass out in terror. She might be wearing lipstick, but twelve was still awfully young.

He nodded to the older woman behind the table. "I'll have some champagne."

The woman looked at him blankly. "I think there's punch in the bowl."

Robert looked over and saw the punch. It was pink.

"I don't suppose there's any bottled water?"

The woman shook her head no. "There might be coffee later."

Robert nodded. He'd have to do this empty-handed. He walked over to the girl. She was leaning against the side of the barn and watching the other kids sort through some old records. Now who had those relics? He couldn't remember ever seeing records played. Not with cassettes and CDs available.

"Know any musicians?"

The girl looked up and shook her head shyly. "Do you?"

Robert nodded. He'd be able to score a few points with this one. "Name a group and I probably know them."

He realized when he said it that it was true. The world of the truly famous was pathetically small.

"Elvis," the girl named softly.

"Elvis is dead."

"I thought maybe you had known him. When you were young."

Robert wondered if he'd fallen down a time warp. "How old do you think I am?"

The girl shrugged. "He's my favorite is all."

"He'll always be the King," Robert agreed gently. Maybe this girl wasn't the one, after all. Her eyes reminded him of Bambi. He didn't want to see the confusion in them that would surely come if a man as old as Elvis kissed her.

"You got a camera?" he asked instead.

"A disposable one."

"Do me a favor and take a few pictures of me tonight. I'll tell you when."

"Sure."

Robert nodded his thanks. Tabloids loved pictures like that and even sweet-eyed Bambis needed a college fund. Somebody might as well get some good out of tonight.

The lights in the barn were subdued and the whole place seemed to smell of butter and steam. Long tables were set up in the back of the barn and covered with white cotton tablecloths. Stacks of heavy plates, the kind found in truck stops, stood at the end of each table.

Several teams of ranch hands were holding big trays with a towel draped over steaming lobsters. Robert frowned at the men. Why hadn't Jenny asked him to help? He'd had to practically demand a knife and some carrots earlier.

Jenny put a dozen silver tongs down on the head table and blessed Mrs. Buckwalter for requesting that they be brought to Dry Creek along with dozens of tiny silver lobster picks. Even Jenny wasn't sure she'd tackle the lobster dinner with plastic forks and no tongs. "Can someone go back and get the last pan of butter?"

"I'll do it."

Jenny stopped arranging the tongs and looked up in panic. It was Robert Buckwalter. "But you can't—I mean you don't need to—"

"Well, someone needs to."

"I can do it myself," Jenny said. She could at least try to remember the difference in their social standing. He was, after all, her employer's son. "You don't want to spill butter on that suit. It looks expensive." Jenny took a deep breath and smiled. Her sister owed her for this one. "I mean, it's a tuxedo, isn't it? Good enough to wear to a wedding."

"Tonight's a special occasion."

"Aren't they all?" She struggled upstream. "These receptions—nothing brings out the good suits like a reception or a wedding."

Robert nodded. "Or a funeral."

Jenny started to sweat. Being a news source was more difficult than one would think. "Funerals and weddings. Sometimes it's hard to tell the difference."

Robert looked at her like she'd lost her mind.

"I mean sometimes weddings get off to a rocky start." Boy, did her sister owe her.

Robert nodded. "I suppose so."

"Been to any weddings lately?"

Robert shrugged. "Not for a while. I've been away from the social scene."

"Oh?" Jenny looked up brightly. Now they were getting somewhere.

"Haven't missed it." Robert looked toward the barn door. "It won't take me a minute to run back to the café and get that butter."

Jenny nodded in defeat. "It's on the back of the stove. Be sure and use a pot holder." She suddenly remembered to whom she was talking. "That's a padded square of cloth. It'll be on the counter."

"I know what a pot holder is." Robert didn't add that he hadn't known until five months ago.

Jenny stood with her back to the tables and watched Robert walk out of the barn. He was limping. Now she wondered why a man who had spent five months resting would be limping.

"Handsome, isn't he?"

Jenny turned to look at the woman standing next to her. Mrs. Hargrove was one of the people in Dry Creek that Jenny liked the best. She'd organized the apron brigade for Jenny, using aprons from the church. Towel aprons. Frilly aprons. Patched aprons. They'd used them all.

"You're pretty good-looking yourself," Jenny said.

The older woman had worn a gingham cotton

dress every other time Jenny had seen her. Tonight she was in a silk mauve dress with a strand of pearls around her neck. A lemon scent floated around her.

"Maybe he'll ask you to dance," Jenny continued. Mrs. Hargrove had said earlier that this was the first dance she'd attended since her husband died two years ago.

"Me?" Mrs. Hargrove laughed. "I was thinking he'd ask you to dance."

"No time. I'll be busy with the food."

"Not when the dancing starts."

"No, by then I'll be busy with the pots and pans—washing dishes."

"Goodness, no! The dishes can wait. Tomorrow's soon enough for that. We'll all pitch in then. That's the way it's done here. I might even ask old man Gossett to help us. Be good for him to get out. You'd be doing him a favor."

Jenny had a sudden wish that she could dance. "But I'm not dressed for a party."

Mrs. Hargrove shrugged. "I'll bet there's a few more dresses at the café."

The women of Dry Creek had loaned their old prom dresses and bridesmaids dresses to the teenage girls from Seattle. For most of the girls, this was the first time in their lives they had worn a formal dress.

"He's back," the older woman announced.

Robert Buckwalter entered the barn doorway and stood for a moment. Jenny could see the blackness of the outside air. Snowflakes were scattered on his head and shoulders. His hands were carefully wrapped around the handle of the saucepan he was holding. He hesitated in the doorway as though he was shy, unsure of his place among the guests. His shyness, combined with the perfect balance of his face almost took her breath away. Maybe he did deserve to be the number one bachelor.

He certainly didn't deserve to carry the butter.

"Here, let me get that." Jenny wiped her hands on her apron and started toward him. The steam from the lobsters had made her hands clammy. "You shouldn't have to—"

"I can carry a pan of butter."

"Of course." Jenny stopped. Of course he could. Why in the world was she so nervous around the man? It must be her sister. Making him sound so mysterious. Just because he was rich, it didn't mean he wasn't just a regular kind of a guy, too. He just had more change in his pockets than most.

"Dinner's almost ready." Jenny turned to talk again with Mrs. Hargrove.

The regular guy walked around her toward the table.

"Then your troubles for the evening will be over," Mrs. Hargrove said kindly as she put a hand on Jenny's arm. "We're so grateful for all the work you've done, dear."

Robert frowned as he set the saucepan on the table. If dinner was coming soon, he had work to do fast. He suspected people were always more easily shocked on an empty stomach. Plus, after dinner, the sounds of those records playing would mask his attempts at being outrageous.

He'd given some thought to his dilemma while outside and he'd decided age could go two ways. Instead of focusing on someone young like Bambi, he could try someone old enough to be his grandmother.

"Ah, there you are." Robert turned back to Mrs. Hargrove. He understood she was the Sunday school teacher for most of the little people in Dry Creek. She should be thoroughly offended by a kiss from a strange man. Everyone else should be shocked, too.

He looked around for Bambi and called her over. There'd be no point in rattling the people of Dry Creek if he couldn't shake up the rest of the country, too.

"Yes?" Mrs. Hargrove looked up at him. Her eyes were bright with curiosity. Her cheeks were pink. She must be seventy years old. She looked like every cookie-lover's picture of Grandma.

Robert dove right in. "I love you."

"Why, I love you, too." She beamed back.

"What?" Robert stalled. This wasn't the way it was supposed to go.

"I love all of God's children," Mrs. Hargrove

continued. "They say that's how Christians will know each other. By the love they have for others. I John 4:7. Does this mean you're a Christian?"

"Well, no, I—I mean I'm not opposed to Christianity." Robert started to sweat in earnest. How had God gotten into this? "Don't really even know much about it—"

"Well, I'd be happy to tell you."

"Great, maybe later. It's just that's not what I meant when I said I love you."

"Well, then, what did you mean?"

Robert was desperate. He looked over and nodded at Bambi. She was in position. Then he started to bend down.

Unfortunately, Mrs. Hargrove bent, too. "My beads."

Robert heard the scattered dropping of pearls as his kiss landed smack on the top of Mrs. Hargrove's gray head. His lips met the scalp where her hair was parted.

"Oh, dear," Mrs. Hargrove said as she bent down farther.

Now Robert couldn't even kiss the top of her head unless he squatted down to where his kneecaps should be.

"Here, let me help you," Jenny said as she stepped closer to both of them.

Robert wasn't about to give up. It wasn't ideal.

But the camera was in place and he was determined to kiss someone. Even if it was Jenny.

He heard her first soft shocked breath as he drew Jenny to him. He was close enough to feel her second indignant breath as he bent his head.

The camera flashed. The talking stopped. A bead rolled.

Robert was triumphant. His big moment was recorded. He could end the kiss. But he didn't. Something was happening.

The kiss blossomed. Jenny tasted of home. The minute Robert felt her lips tremble beneath his, he was lost. He didn't want the kiss to end. He felt like he had caught a fragile thread of something precious he didn't even understand.

"Mmmm, sweet. I like that—I mean you—I like you," he whispered when he finally drew away.

"Not love?" Bright red dots stood out on both of Jenny's cheeks. "I thought 'I love you' came easy enough to your type."

Robert felt like he was coming out of a cozy cave and facing the frost of winter.

"My type?" he asked cautiously.

Jenny's brown eyes had deepened to a snapping black. She bristled.

"The type of man who kisses his employees— whom he *likes*—even when he says he loves Mrs. Hargrove."

"I don't kiss my employ—" Robert stopped.

That was no longer true. "I mean, I don't. Well, I didn't—"

There was an incessant ringing somewhere and a gnarled old hand reached from behind Robert. Mr. Gossett had pulled the ringing phone out of the coat pocket. "This yours?"

"You want it?" Robert asked Jenny.

Jenny's cheeks were red still and her breathing quick. She was adorable.

Robert suspected she reached for the phone more for something to do than because she wanted to talk.

"Yes." Jenny turned her back to him and walked a few feet away.

"You talked to him!" She looked over her shoulder in a betraying move. It was the sister. "So he knows."

Robert knew he should pick up on the accusation Jenny had left dangling and make some strong sexual harassment statements. Publicly threaten to fire her unless she kissed him again. That would certainly knock him off the bachelor list. Women didn't tolerate sexual harassment anymore and they shouldn't.

But Robert didn't open his mouth. Suddenly the list was not all that important.

He had met the woman the Bob inside him wanted to marry and she was looking at him this very minute like he was some hair ball a very unwelcome stray cat had coughed up.

Considering the set of her jaw as she talked to her sister, Robert figured he had as much chance of ever kissing her again as he had of teaching that stray cat to dance a tango.

Chapter Three

"He kissed you! You're telling me he kissed you! Robert Buckwalter the Third kissed you!"

Jenny's sister was screeching so loudly Jenny had to hold the cell phone away from her ear. She'd slipped outside so that she could finish the phone conversation in private. She shivered from the cold.

"After he kissed Mrs. Hargrove," Jenny said as she wiped one hand on her chef's apron. The coarse bleached muslin steadied her. She was a chef. An employee. "He's my boss. He can't kiss me. He didn't even say he loved me."

"Love! He loves you!" her sister screeched even louder.

"No, he didn't say that—that's what I'm saying. He didn't even attempt to be sincere."

"But he kissed you."

The Montana night was lit by some stars and a perfectly round moon. Silver shadows fell on the snow where the reflection of the barn light showed through the barn door and two square side windows. A jumble of cars and trucks were parked in the road leading up to the barn.

"Maybe he did it because I talked to you about him. Maybe there's some servant's code I breached when I told secrets about the master. You know, maybe it's a revenge thing."

Jenny could hear the pause on the other end of the phone. The silence lasted for a full minute.

Finally her sister spoke. "Have you been taking those vitamins Mom sent you?"

"Well, yes, but what does that have to do with anything?"

"You're getting old. First you don't even wonder about whether or not the man is married and now he kisses you—Robert Buckwalter the Third actually kisses you—and you think it's for revenge!"

"Well, it could be."

"Men like him don't kiss for revenge! They use lawsuits. Or buyouts. Corporate takeovers. They use termination. He could fire you. But not kisses! Kisses are for romance."

Jenny snorted. "I smell like fish and my hair is flat. No man's kissing me for romance."

"You're in your chef's apron?" Some of the bubble drained out of her sister's voice. "With that funny hair net on?"

"And orthopedic white shoes because I'm standing so much. And no makeup because the steam from the lobster pots would make my mascara run. And I even have a butter stain on my apron—not a big one, but it's there in the left corner."

"Then why is he kissing you?" her sister wailed and then caught herself. "Not that—I mean you're real attractive when you're…well, you know—"

"Those are my thoughts exactly. I might pass for someone in his social circle when I'm dressed up— heels, makeup, the works."

"You looked real good in that black dress you wore last New Year's."

"But in my working clothes, I'm more likely to attract a raving lunatic than a rich man."

"Are you sure you don't have some exotic perfume on? One of those musk oil scents?"

"Not a drop."

"Well, this isn't fair, then. A man like this Buckwalter fellow shouldn't go around kissing women just for kicks. He could hurt their feelings."

"That's what I'm trying to tell you. He's so rich he doesn't need to worry about anyone's feelings. Especially the feelings of his employees."

It was the dumped pet thing all over again. The rich were rich enough to be selfish. They didn't care about their pets. They didn't care about other people.

That was all there was to it. The normal courtesies of life didn't apply to people like Robert Buckwalter.

Jenny looked over toward the barn. Mrs. Hargrove stood in the open doorway watching her anxiously. She was motioning for her to come back inside.

"I think they need me." Jenny waved Mrs. Hargrove back into the warm barn. "It must be lobster time. Talk to you later."

"Call me."

"I will—wait." She'd just thought of something. "When you talked to Robert Buckwalter earlier, did you tell him he was number one on the list or did you just say you were thinking of making him number one?"

"Oh, I couldn't tell him he was number one. I said maybe, but I didn't say it had been settled. That's not decided. Besides, it's confidential."

"I see. Thanks. I'll call you later."

Jenny slipped the cell phone into the front pocket of her chef's apron. Well, that explained everything. Robert Buckwalter thought a kiss might nudge him into that first-place position. Cozy up to the sister of someone with influence on the list and—presto—he's at the top. It was a game as old as mankind.

The heat inside the barn enfolded Jenny when she stepped across the threshold. She rubbed her arms. She'd been so angry she hadn't noticed the goose bumps that had crept up her arms. It was freezing outside.

"There you are, dear," Mrs. Hargrove said. The older woman stepped toward her. "I was worried. I forgot to tell you that there's been a threat of kidnapping tonight. Garth Elkton has cautioned all the women to stay inside."

"A kidnapping? Here?"

Jenny looked around in astonishment. She couldn't imagine a less likely place for a kidnapping. The teenagers had strung pink and white crepe paper from the rafters, making Jenny feel as if she were trapped in Candy Land. Dozens of ranchers and their wives sat at the long white tables at the back of the barn. Some of the ranchers had arms as big as wrestlers. What kind of army would it take to kidnap someone from here tonight?

"But who—?" Jenny asked.

"Garth Elkton got a strange call warning him that someone was out to get his sister."

"Francis!" Jenny had met the woman earlier and liked her instantly. "But who would want to kidnap her?"

Mrs. Hargrove leaned close. "Some folks say it's an old boyfriend of hers. But I don't believe them. Flint Harris is a good boy. I always thought Dry Creek would be proud of him one day."

Jenny looked over at the string of men standing along the far side of the barn. Most of them wore dark cowboy work boots and had the raw look of a new shave on their faces. "Which one is he?"

"Why, none of them, dear. Flint Harris hasn't been in Dry Creek for almost twenty years now."

"Well, then, surely he's not a threat."

Mrs. Hargrove shrugged. "I've never believed he was. Everyone's so wound up about this cattle rustling that's going on that we're making fools of ourselves, I'm afraid. Folks are saying now that the FBI thinks that someone from Dry Creek is tipping off the cattle rustlers. Imagine that! It's rattled a lot of folks, but I don't set much store by it. It'll all blow over. But it's best that you be careful. If you need to go over to the café, let me know and I'll get one of the ranch hands to go with you."

Jenny nodded. "I think we have everything we need to get started."

Steam from the lobsters kept the air inside the barn moist and Jenny could smell the coffee someone had set to brew.

Mrs. Buckwalter took charge, thanking everyone for coming and asking Matthew Curtis, the newly married minister, to say a blessing on the celebration meal. He agreed and asked everyone to join hands.

Jenny offered one hand to Mrs. Hargrove and the other to a young girl with rosy cheeks standing next to her.

The whole town of Dry Creek held hands and then closed their eyes.

"For the blessings You have given, we thank You, Lord," the minister prayed. He held the hand of his new bride, a fresh-faced redhead that people had been calling Angel all night long. "For this food eaten with friends, we are most grateful. Keep us in Your love. Amen."

"And thanks for my money, too," the young girl at Jenny's side whispered quietly, her eyes still squeezed shut.

Jenny hadn't noticed that the girl wasn't holding someone's hand on the other side of her. Instead she was clutching a green piece of paper that looked like a check.

"Maybe you should put that with your coat." Jenny nodded her head in the general direction of a few chairs near the door that were haphazardly piled with coats. "You wouldn't want to lose your allowance."

"I don't get an allowance," the girl whispered. "But I don't need one now, because I'm rich."

"We've got a lot to be grateful for." Jenny smiled down at the girl. What did it matter if the girl kept her few dollars in her hand if it made her feel better?

"I'm especially grateful for him," the girl whispered again.

Jenny followed the girl's gaze and it led her straight to the tuxedoed back of—

"Robert Buckwalter!" Jenny looked down at the

girl in alarm. The sweet young thing's face glowed in adoration. "What's he done to you?"

Jenny looked at the broad shoulders of the man who was causing trouble. It wasn't enough that he'd kissed Jenny and Mrs. Hargrove, he'd obviously kissed others, too.

Robert looked perfectly at ease, talking with a couple of teenage boys who were fidgeting with their ties. It almost looked like he was giving them a lesson in how to make a tie bearable.

Jenny wished he would turn around and face her. It wasn't nearly as satisfying to scowl at a man's back as it would be to scowl at his face.

Folding chairs had been pulled close to the long table. People everywhere were walking toward the chairs and sitting down.

Jenny looked over and caught the eye of one of the ranch hands. She nodded for him to begin serving the lobsters like they had arranged earlier.

"I'll be right with you." Jenny was in charge of bringing the melted butter to the table, but it would take a minute for the lobsters to make the rounds and she had something to do before she served it.

"Excuse me," Jenny said. Her eyes were level with the back shoulder of Robert Buckwalter and she could feel the stiffness in her own spine. That poor innocent girl was no match for a man like this and Jenny felt she must protest his flirtation with her.

The man turned around. "Jenny!"

Jenny almost stumbled. The man said her name with joy.

"I know this is a party—" Jenny kept her eyes focused on Robert Buckwalter's chin. She didn't want to lose her nerve. She had stuck up for her younger siblings for years. She'd stick up for that young girl. "—and a dance at that. But you're an adult and you have to know that a child—well, you're old enough to be her father and I think you should remember that."

"I'm old enough to be whose father?"

Jenny lifted her gaze from his chin to his eyes. If she didn't know better, she would say he was puzzled. And his eyes were distracting. A clear sky blue. They made her dizzy and annoyed at the same time.

"All of them," she snapped. "You're old enough to be father to all of the kids here."

"Well, that's stretching it, but if it makes you feel better, I assure you I'm not father to anyone—especially no one in this room."

"You shouldn't kiss them then."

Jenny kept her voice low. She hadn't forgotten about the teenage boys who were standing close enough to hear what she was saying if she wasn't careful.

Robert had no such need for privacy. "Kissing? When?"

Suddenly the air became supercharged.

"Kissing!" A teenage boy yelled out and then gave a piercing basketball whistle. "Hey everybody—he's gonna kiss her again!"

Jenny paled and she looked back at Robert. His eyes had deepened from sky blue to a midnight blue. And he was starting to grin.

"You shouldn't have mentioned kisses," he said.

"What's going on?" Jenny felt as if she'd landed in a science-fiction movie. She turned around. She was suddenly surrounded by twenty, maybe thirty teenagers and they were all noisily aiming cheap disposable cameras at her.

"I suppose we should blame my mother. She bought them the cameras so they could take pictures of the wildlife in Montana."

"But what do they want with us? We don't even live in Montana. I grew up in Seattle. I don't even know what the wildlife here looks like. I've never seen an elk, or a mountain sheep, or—"

"I think," Robert said, as he touched her shoulders and turned her around until she was facing him again, "they want to see this."

Robert dipped his head toward her and Jenny's heart stopped. She knew he meant to kiss her. It was obvious. But she couldn't move. She meant to move. Her mind assured her of that. It was her feet. Her feet had betrayed her and turned to stone.

Robert's lips met hers and Jenny's feet melted.

She could hardly stand. She put her arms on his shoulders more for support than anything.

Ahhh. It was sweet. Very sweet.

Jenny felt like she went to a distant place where there was nothing but this man kissing her. Everything else was fuzzy. Then she saw a bright light. And heard a faint click. Then another click. This is it, she thought. Her heart was giving out. The end was always described as coming with a bright light. She wasn't sure about the clicking. She should have paid more attention in Sunday school. She bet Mrs. Hargrove knew about the clicking. Jenny only hoped it didn't have anything to do with that other place. Could it be fire crackling? She really should have paid more attention.

Then the light wavered and Jenny blinked.

The kiss stopped.

She glanced up and saw his face. Robert Buckwalter looked as stunned as she felt.

"It's the cameras," Jenny finally whispered. She wasn't dying, after all.

"I heard bells."

"No, it was just the clicking." Jenny pulled away from him slightly so she could check her feet.

Her feet would work, Jenny assured herself as she pulled away farther. She suddenly needed more room. "I've got to see to the butter."

"Are you going for it again?" one of the teenage

boys yelled out. "I've still got five shots left on my camera. Might as well fill it up."

"Yeah, me, too," another boy added.

"I heard bells," Robert Buckwalter repeated slowly.

"You heard clicking," Jenny said forcefully. She took a deep breath. "To you it sounded like bells. To me it sounded like the fires of..." She took another quick breath. "Just how gullible do you think I am? I'm not doing anything about that list, so you can just forget this—this—" Jenny waved her hand, but could not finish the sentence. This what? This earthquake? This landslide? Everything seemed more something than simply this kiss.

"Besides, I have the butter to serve," Jenny said with dignity as she pulled herself away. She congratulated herself. Her feet worked perfectly well.

The lobsters were all eaten and the butter dishes empty before Robert felt free to escape from the party and sit on the steps leading out of the barn door.

He was a mess. Some love song was filling the barn with swaying rhythm and dozens of couples were dancing together. He should be dancing. He should be in there dancing with the woman who had turned him inside out, but he wasn't. Jenny was bustling around making sure everyone had coffee. Everyone, that is, except him. He was sure she wouldn't offer him any even if he stood in front of her like a beggar with an empty cup.

One thing was clear—Jenny had little use for Robert Buckwalter. What wasn't clear was if she could love Bob instead.

"Mind if I join you?"

Robert looked up to see Matthew Curtis, the minister, coming out of the barn.

"Help yourself." Robert moved over on the steps. The steps were wooden and had been swept clean of snow even though they were still cold enough to make a man notice when he was changing spots. "There's room for both of us on these steps."

"I could get us chairs from inside," Matthew offered as he turned to go back in the barn. "That's what I should do—get us some nice folding chairs."

"I haven't seen anyone else use folding chairs."

"Well, we don't, but you're—"

"I'm what?"

Robert wondered how much trouble he could get in if he took a swing at a minister. "Go ahead, tell me. I'm what?"

The night air was damp. Snow wasn't falling, but the air was heavy with the promise of a blizzard later. Clouds covered most of the stars and half of the moon.

Matthew turned and stepped down next to Robert. "I'd guess right now you're a man who's just feeling bad. Want to talk about it?"

Robert realized he did. "You might not understand how it is with me."

"No, probably not," Matthew agreed as he settled onto the steps. "Can't say I've ever had the problems of a rich man."

"What makes you think it's got to do with money?"

Matthew shrugged. "Just a guess. You're rich. That's got to be a burden—although I'd guess it's a little less of a burden after tonight."

Robert looked at him.

"All those rolls of film you bought from the kids must have set you back a pretty penny. I heard them saying you were paying one thousand dollars for each picture they got of you kissing Jenny. I heard them cameras each take twenty-four shots. One of the kids is still kicking himself for taking three shots of the decorations before you started your kissing. Can't blame him. I almost got a camera myself and started taking pictures. That's going to be a half-million-dollar kiss when you've paid off all the kids."

"Does Jenny know about this?" Robert wasn't so sure he wanted her to find out about this when she was carrying around a pot of hot coffee. She might be inclined to throw some of it his way without benefit of a cup.

"No. The kids are keeping quiet like you asked. They're tiptoeing around her. But they're so excited, they're going to burst if they don't tell someone. I'd guess a few of the adults know. And they're all wondering why—"

"It seemed like a good idea." Robert paused. The air was cold enough to make puff clouds of his breath. "It started with Bambi. I thought she should go to college someday."

Matthew nodded. "You're a generous man. That should make you feel good."

"It should."

"But it doesn't?"

"It's not enough. The way I see it, I'm missing something."

Matthew nodded. "Go on."

"I have too many friends. No, that's not right. They're not really friends. They're only people who like me because I'm rich. Because I have all the toys. Each one of those kids in there has a better friend and is a better friend to someone than I am. That's a hard realization to come to. If I died, it's not me people would miss, it's my toys."

"You planning on dying?"

"Well, no, not anytime soon." Robert realized it was hard to pin down the hollow feeling he had. "But if I did—"

Matthew nodded again. "What's troubling you is that you need to be part of the kingdom and you're not."

Robert stopped. He'd heard there were militia

groups in Montana. He wondered if he'd stumbled across one. They'd sure love to recruit a rich man like him who could buy them enough ammunition to start a small war.

"The kingdom?" Robert asked cautiously.

"Sure, the kingdom of God," Matthew said calmly. "It's all that will fill up that empty feeling. When you're ready, we'll talk about it."

"I don't think it has to do with God."

Matthew grinned as he stood. "I know. You think it all has to do with that cute chef inside who's in need of a dance. If you don't ask her, somebody else is going to beat you to it."

"She won't dance with me."

Matthew grinned even wider. "Well, maybe not the first time you ask her. But you're Robert Buckwalter the Third. Way I hear it, you know about all there is about charming women."

The minister stepped inside the barn and Robert stood up and brushed himself off before following him.

The minister was right. He did know how to charm women. He just wasn't sure charm would work with someone like Jenny.

The music was softer now. Even the kids were slowing down.

Robert went over to the refreshment table and got a glass of punch to work up his nerve. Jenny was still flitting about filling up coffee cups for those people who were sitting around the edge of the dance space and talking. He'd studied her pattern. She needed to return to the refreshment table to refill her thermal pot after every tenth cup. She was due back any minute now.

When she came back, he would ask her to dance with him.

Chapter Four

"Well, I hope you're happy now," Jenny said as she set the thermal coffeepot down on the refreshment table and glared at Robert Buckwalter. "Throwing your money around like it's confetti."

Robert stiffened. He looked around at the teenagers dancing. He hoped no one had told her what he was buying with the money. None of the dancers were looking at him in apology. "No one else is complaining."

"Of course they're not complaining." Jenny turned to the big coffeepot and twisted the knob on its spigot so it would slowly fill the smaller thermal coffeepot. The mellow smell of brewed coffee drifted up from the pot. She looked up and continued her conversation. "What do you expect? They're teenagers. They love money."

"Money has its uses."

Jenny switched off the knob. The small pot was full. And she was tired to the bone. She'd been a fool. There for a blinding moment she'd thought Robert Buckwalter was a regular kind of a guy who just happened to be rich. What kind of rabbit hole had she fallen down? She should know better. No one just happened to be rich. Money changed everyone. "Not everything in the world revolves around money."

"I know."

"You can't buy friends with money—not even the friendship of teenagers." After Jenny said the words, she corrected herself. Those teenagers certainly spoke of Robert with enough enthusiasm to count him a friend. And the checks were awfully big. She'd seen one of them.

Robert grinned. The kids had managed to keep his secret. Jenny didn't know why he'd been throwing checks around. "I didn't give them the money so they'd be my friends."

"Well, with the size of those checks—they should be something."

"I'm hoping they will be something someday."

Jenny looked at him suspiciously.

"Something for themselves. I'm hoping they'll go to college—maybe learn a trade—be good citizens," Robert explained. "Grow up to be their own something. What's wrong with that?"

Jenny was silent for a moment. "Nothing."

Her sister was right, Jenny thought in defeat. She, Jenny M. Black, was turning into one of those fussy old women. Picking a fight with a perfectly innocent man just because he'd given away some of his money. And that wasn't even the real reason. The real reason was the kiss. And that was just as foolish. In his social circles, a kiss was nothing more than a handshake.

"Who you give money to is none of my business," Jenny said stiffly as she put the lid back on the small coffeepot. "I owe you an apology."

"I'll take a dance instead." Robert held his breath. He'd seen the loophole and dived through it, but it wasn't a smooth move. He'd done better courting when he was sixteen. He had no polish left. He was reduced to the bare truth. "I've been hoping you'd save a dance for me."

Jenny looked at him like he was crazy. "Save a dance? Me? I'm not dancing."

"And why not?"

Jenny held up the coffeepot. She hated to point out the obvious. "I'm here to see that others have a good time. That's what your mother pays me to do and I intend to do it. I, for one, believe in earning my money."

"I could pa—" Robert started to tease and then stopped. He didn't know how she'd twist his offer to pay for a dance, but he could see trouble snapping in her eyes already. "My mother doesn't expect you to wait on people all night."

Robert looked over to where his mother was talking with Mrs. Hargrove. They were sitting on two folding chairs by the door to the barn. If his mother wasn't so intent on the conversation, he knew she would have already come over and told Jenny to take it easy.

"You're not going to ask her, are you?" Jenny looked horrified.

"Not if you don't want me to. But if you're so determined to give people coffee. I could pass some around for you. With two of us working, it'd take half the time. How much coffee can everyone drink?"

"I can manage."

"No one should be drinking coffee at this time of night anyway." Robert wondered if he'd completely lost his touch. She shouldn't still be frowning at him. Any other woman would be untying those apron strings and smiling at him by now.

"It's decaf."

"Still. There's all this punch." Robert gestured to the half-full bowl of pink punch. The color of the punch had faded as the evening wore on, and the ice had melted. The plastic dipper was half floating in the liquid. "Pity to see it go to waste."

"The punch drinkers are all dancing." Jenny looked out at the dance floor wistfully. The only people left drinking coffee were the single men, mostly the ranch hands from Garth Elkton's place. The teenagers had downed many a cup of punch after dinner, but they were all dancing now.

Robert followed her gaze. "The kids are doing their best, aren't they?"

The swish of taffeta skirts rustled all along the dance floor. A long, slow sixties love song whispered low and throaty from the record player. Most of the teenagers were paired up and dancing with a determined concentration that Robert applauded. He even saw one or two of the boys try a dip with their partners. Now that was courage.

"They remind me of an old Fred Astaire and Ginger Rogers movie—all those colors swirling around."

The old prom dresses were lavender, slate gray, buttercup yellow, forest green, primrose pink—and they all seemed to have full skirts that trailed on the plank flooring of the barn. Their skirts reminded Jenny of a bed of pansies.

"We could be swirling, too—" Robert held out one hand for the coffeepot and the other for Jenny's hand.

The light in the old barn had been softened when the music started. Someone had turned off a few of the side lights and shadows crowded the tall corners of the structure. The air was cool and, by the sounds of it, a winter wind was blowing outside.

When Jenny had looked outside earlier, she'd thought that the snow falling in the black night looked like a snow globe turned upside down—with the barn at the center and an old-fashioned waltz playing while the snow fell around the globe.

"I can't dance in this." Jenny brought her mind back to reality. She gestured to her chef's apron. Her broad white apron was serviceable for working with food, but it had nothing of taffeta or silk about it. Even Ginger didn't dance in coarse cotton. "And there's my hair—"

"Your hair is beautiful. You just need to get rid of this." Robert reached over and lifted Jenny's hair net off her head.

Jenny's hands flew up. "But that's my hair net— the health code."

"No one needs a hair net for dancing."

No, Jenny thought, but they did need air in their lungs. She felt dizzy. She could almost hear her sister's squeal of delight if she knew Robert Buckwalter had plucked the net off her hair and asked her to dance.

But Jenny had always been more practical than her sister.

Jenny knew that Prince Charming didn't even notice Cinderella until after the Fairy Godmother had given her a whole new look. Men, especially handsome men like the one in front of her, just didn't dance with women with working shoes and flat hair.

Not even the coachmen would have danced with Cinderella if she'd arrived at the ball with a net over her hair and an apron around her waist.

"I should change."

Jenny's hand had already found its way into his and now she was twisting away from him to go do something as foolish as change her clothes.

"You're fine." Fine didn't begin to cover it, Robert thought to himself. Jenny's eyes, usually a dark brown, had lightened to a caramel. She had a dazed look about her that made him want to dance with her in a quiet corner instead of in the middle of a throng of teenagers.

It wasn't that she was beautiful, he decided after a moment. He'd seen dozens of women whose features were more perfect. But he'd never seen anyone who looked like Jenny. He could almost trace her thoughts in her eyes. She wasn't trying to hide who she was or what she thought. He wondered if she even knew how rare that was. Or how compelling.

"But my hair..." Jenny frantically tried to fluff her hair up a little. It was all about bone structure. With flat hair, the small features on her face made her look like a Christmas elf. With just a little bit of fluff, she managed to look merely petite instead of childish.

Robert captured her hand and calmed her.

"Your hair is—" He'd been going to say "fine."

But then he felt the cloud of her hair fall against the back of his hand. "—incredible."

"It's brown." Jenny shook her hair away from his hand. No wonder he was in the running for the number one bachelor. He was a charmer, all right. "Plain brown and flyaway on top of that."

Robert shook his head. "I'd say more chestnut than anything, golden highlights. The kind of hair the masters used to paint in all those old European pictures. Mona Lisa colors."

"Next you'll be saying my apron is the latest fashion from Paris."

Robert could see the amusement begin in her eyes and he could feel her relaxing.

"Just see if it doesn't catch on." Robert guided her closer so they could waltz. He felt her momentary resistance before she moved toward him.

"I used to love to dance." Maybe the shadows will hide my apron, Jenny thought to herself as Robert started them on their way.

"Ever dip?"

Jenny shook her head. "And don't you dare. I'd feel foolish with everyone looking."

"Everybody's too busy to care."

Jenny looked around at the other couples. It was true. Almost. "The ranch hands are watching."

Robert looked at the cluster of men standing by one of the side heaters. Half of them held coffee cups in their hands. A few of them did seem to be looking at him and Jenny, although he'd wager they weren't interested in her apron. The dismay he saw in the eyes of a couple of them told him they'd been waiting for the coffee passing to stop so they'd have their own chance at a dance with Jenny.

"They'll just have to get their own dates," Robert stated firmly as he gathered Jenny a little closer and inhaled. She smelled of some very pleasing scent. He'd guess cinnamon.

Jenny almost stumbled. "Date?"

Robert looked down at her face and smiled. "You. Me. Dancing. That's a date, isn't it?"

"But we can't be on a date." Jenny stopped dancing.

"Why not?"

"You're my boss."

"I've never paid you a dime. You work for my mother."

"It's the same difference," Jenny sputtered. "Besides—" she hated to sound like her sister, but there it was "—I'm Jenny, the chef, and you're Robert Buckwalter the Third."

"You can call me Bob."

"What?" Jenny hadn't realized how close Robert had pulled her until she'd stopped dancing.

"Bob. Call me Bob."

Jenny looked up at him skeptically. He smelled faintly of some expensive aftershave. The tie around his neck was pure silk and probably Italian. His suit had to be hand tailored. "You don't look like a Bob."

Robert gently started Jenny dancing again. He liked the way she felt in his arms. Her head reached his chin. Not too tall. Not too short. Just right. "What does a Bob look like anyway?"

Jenny was silent a moment. "Plaid shirt. Sneakers."

Robert started to chuckle. "I can't do much about the shirt right now, but I left my sneakers in the bus when we drove over. I could go get them if it'd make you happy. We could both go."

"It's dark out there."

"The stars are out."

"Mrs. Hargrove said we're supposed to stay close to the barn." Jenny tried to hold on to her propriety.

Jenny remembered how soft the black sky was outside. Shadows layered over shadows amid the cars and trucks parked in the middle of Dry Creek. The bite of the air would be cold and sharp enough to make the inside of the bus a cozy place to talk. A much too cozy place when all was said and done.

"She's just worried about that kidnapping rumor." Robert watched the temptation play across Jenny's face. He could watch her for hours. "But only a fool would kidnap anyone in a cold spell like the one tonight. There's three feet of snow out there in some places."

"I suppose."

Robert noticed the frown didn't go away. "If you're worried about me, don't be. I'm a gentleman. You can trust me."

Jenny snapped back to reality. "You're not a gentleman. You're the bachelor of the year."

Robert came back to reality with her. "I am? Have you talked to your sister? Have they decided?"

"No."

"The whole thing is cruel and unusual punishment."

Jenny nodded. She supposed the waiting and suspense did seem like that to him. He must really want the slot. "My sister says the winner will be able to write his own ticket with the advertising companies."

Robert groaned. "I'd forgotten about that part of it. I may need to fly Charlie in to take those calls after all."

"Who's Charlie? Your attorney?"

Robert started to chuckle. "No, Charlie is an acquaintance of another kind."

"Oh." Don't tell me he has an agent, Jenny thought in dismay. He certainly had the looks to go into modeling. But somehow, she was disappointed. "I hope you draw the line at underwear."

Robert blinked. "Underwear?"

"You know, in the endorsements. I wouldn't want to see you in a magazine in your underwear."

Jenny felt the blush creep up her neck. He didn't have to look at her that way—like she was picturing him right now in his underwear. "I just think it wouldn't be a good example for the kids around here."

"You're worried they'll grow up to be underwear salesmen?" Robert was entranced. He'd seen precious few blushes in his day. That must say something about the kind of woman that usually flocked around him.

"Well, it's not very steady work."

"I don't know about that. People always need underwear."

If they hadn't been talking, Jenny was sure she would have noticed that the music had stopped.

She did notice the loud voices from the front of the barn near the door.

A woman's voice called, "Francis? Anyone seen Francis?"

There was a loud shuffling as the boots of the ranch hands who were sitting by the heater hit the floor with a united thud.

A man's rough voice demanded, "Garth? Where's Garth?"

Finally one of the teenage girls opened the barn door from the outside and shrieked, "Kidnapping! They were right! There's a kidnapping! We saw the truck—we saw them!" The girl's face was white, but Jenny couldn't tell if it was from the outside cold or from shock.

"Come in, dear. Tell us what you saw." Mrs. Hargrove was drawing the girl inside as Jenny and Robert arrived at her side.

"Bryan and I were outside looking at the stars when we heard a gunshot."

"I told you that was a gunshot," one of the ranch hands muttered to another.

"Are you sure it was a gunshot?" Mrs. Hargrove put a jacket around the shivering girl. "It might have been a car misfiring."

"But there weren't any cars running. Not even that big truck was going when we heard the shot," the girl insisted. "Besides, I know the difference between a gunshot and a car backfiring."

Mrs. Hargrove took a quick, assessing look at the girl. The girl was tall and skinny with a light brown skin that could signal almost any race. Finally, the older woman nodded. "We'd best call out the sheriff."

"The sheriff? Where's he off to anyway?" one ranch hand said.

"Some guy called in an emergency from the Billings airport," another answered. "Something to do with some VIP."

"I think the guys with the guns are in that big truck that just left," the girl continued. "Bryan saw something shiny that looked like a gun."

"Where's Bryan now?" Robert asked the girl quietly. Something about the whole story didn't seem right to him. Any teenage boy he knew would be in here claiming the glory of the moment. But there was no Bryan.

The girl bit her lip.

Robert looked around. There were a lot more dresses than tuxedoes in the crowd.

"Where's Bryan?" he asked again.

"He wanted to be sure. I told him it was a gunshot, but he wanted to be sure before he told everyone." The girl's brown complexion went a little yellow and she swallowed hard.

"Where is he?"

"He took the bus to follow them."

"Mercy!" Mrs. Hargrove put her hands to her mouth. "When they have guns! And the boy all alone."

"I don't think he's quite all alone," Robert said grimly as he looked over the teenagers again. Then he looked at the girl. "How many other guys are with him?"

The girl looked miserable. "Ten."

"Lord have mercy," Mrs. Hargrove said again.

"We'll have to catch them," Robert said, looking over at the ranch hands. He recognized the men's faces from the ride into Dry Creek on the bus that was now in hot pursuit of the cattle truck. None of them would have a vehicle here. "Who's got a pickup we can borrow?"

"You can take ours," one of the farm wives offered as she bent to fumble in her purse for the keys.

"Anyone call the sheriff yet?" Robert asked as he eyed half a dozen of the ranch hands. "I don't suppose anyone here has a hunting gun in their truck?"

"We called the sheriff," Jenny said with a nod to another one of the ranch women. She held up the cell phone that had been resting in her apron pocket. "But he's tied up at the Billings airport with some woman who came in, named Laurel Carlton or something like that."

"Laurel?" Robert paled. "Here?"

Well, this is it, Jenny thought. Robert certainly looked uncomfortable with the thought of this woman, whoever she was. Maybe her sister was right and he was married after all.

"Fred has a gun," one of the ranch hands yelled from the other side of the barn. "Uses it to scare off coyotes on his place."

"It's an old rifle—draws a little to the left," the man explained as he walked fast toward the door. "But I'll get it. It's better than nothing."

"I think everyone should just wait for the authorities," Mrs. Buckwalter said. "Let them handle it. A gun can be a dangerous thing."

One of the ranch hands snorted. "Tell that to

whoever's in the truck. We can't wait for the sheriff. They'll be long gone by the time he gets here.''

''He's right,'' Robert said.

The farm woman with the pickup pressed a set of keys into the palm of Robert's hand. ''The tank's half-full.''

The other men looked at Robert. He nodded his head at five or six of the sturdiest-looking ones and they, almost in unison, dipped their heads to drop a kiss on their wives' cheeks before starting toward the door.

Now that's what marriage is about, Robert thought to himself. The automatic, comfortable affection of settled love. Having someone to kiss goodbye when you're going off to war or even just heading to the store.

Seeing all those kisses made him feel lonely enough to be brave. What could it hurt?

Jenny was talking to Robert's mother, her head bent slightly to hear his shorter mother. The dark wave of Jenny's hair lay on her neck. Wisps of hair moved with his hand as Robert brushed the hair aside. He hoped to get Jenny's full attention. He'd kissed Mrs. Hargrove on her hair part earlier and had no more appetite for hair kisses.

Jenny looked up. His mother looked up. Satisfied, Robert bent his head to kiss Jenny on her cheek. Her skin was soft as a petal. He could hear her surprised gasp even though it was little more than an indrawn breath.

"I'll be fine," Robert assured Jenny quickly, overlooking the fact that she hadn't asked.

"You're not going with them," Robert's mother said. Jenny still seemed a little dazed. The older woman repeated, "You can't possibly be thinking of going with them."

"I'll be fine." Robert moved to kiss his mother, as well. "Don't worry."

"But they have guns!" Mrs. Buckwalter said, as though that settled everything.

"I'll be back," Robert said as he started to walk toward the door. "Just tell that sheriff to get back here."

"But he can't go." Mrs. Buckwalter repeated the words to Jenny as they watched Robert go through the barn door. A gust of cold wind blew in as the men stepped outside.

"I'm sure he'll be fine." Jenny echoed her son's words for the older woman's benefit.

"But this isn't like him." Mrs. Buckwalter looked at Jenny. "He'd told me he was a changed man, but..." Her voice trailed off. "I thought he meant he was going to move back to Seattle or take up watercolors or get engaged or something sensible—not take off looking for men with guns."

Jenny tried to smile reassuringly. "I'm sure he'll be fine."

Chapter Five

Jenny left the cell phone with Mrs. Buckwalter and walked over to the refreshment table to see how much coffee was left in the big pot. She had a feeling punch wouldn't be enough for the men when they came back.

"The sheriff's coming back as soon as he can," Mrs. Buckwalter reported as she joined Jenny over by the table. "Which probably won't be soon enough to do any good so I called in some of the other authorities around."

Jenny looked up. "I didn't know there was anyone else around here but the county sheriffs."

Mrs. Buckwalter grunted. "There's some fool FBI agent riding around on a horse."

"On a horse!"

"And his boss is here in some kind of a Jeep.

They both travel a bit unconventionally I'm afraid but—''

''I don't care if they get here in a flying saucer,'' Jenny said as she lifted the smaller pot of coffee to start making the rounds. ''Just as long as they get here fast.''

''You're really worried, aren't you?'' Mrs. Buckwalter looked at Jenny as though she were seeing her for the first time.

''Of course.'' Jenny blushed. ''Anyone would be.''

''But you're particularly worried about my son.''

''Only because I know him a little better than the others.''

''I see.'' Mrs. Buckwalter started to smile. ''You know, I've never known my son to kiss a woman on the cheek before.''

Jenny grimaced. She didn't need a reminder. If she ever had any illusions of being irresistible, that kiss certainly dampened them. It wasn't a passionate kiss. A Boy Scout could have done better kissing his grandmother. ''I think he's just trying to be democratic. Being a regular Joe.''

Mrs. Buckwalter looked up questioningly.

''I mean Bob. He wanted me to call him Bob. I think he's trying to be one with the people or something. And he focused on me because I'm—'' she straightened her shoulders ''—because I'm of the class that works for a living.''

"Well, there's nothing wrong with working, dear. I haven't raised Robert to be a snob."

"No, but I can't imagine he has many friends who scrub vegetables for a living. I mean, sure he knows people who work, but they're probably stockbrokers or lawyers or something classy."

"My dear, you're a very classy chef. I dare anyone to make a crème brûlée that surpasses yours," Mrs. Buckwalter said indignantly. "But I don't think it's that at all. I'm beginning to think it's something quite different. He did ask me if I'd brought the family album with me. I was thinking it was because my anniversary would have been next week if my husband had lived. Robert knew I'd have it with me for that day."

"Oh, I'm sorry."

Mrs. Buckwalter smiled wistfully. "My husband's been gone a long time now, but the album brings it all back to me. All three generations of Buckwalters are in the album—my husband and I especially. There are pictures right up to the final anniversary we celebrated seven years ago. My husband just kept adding pages to the thing. The Buckwalter men have a knack for knowing right away the women they want to marry. My husband has a picture of the first time we met—at a charity auction back in 1955. We were both there with other people, but he managed a picture anyway. We were saving something at the time. A local park, I think. Long before it was fashionable to save anything. There we were. It's a picture I treasure.''

"What a lovely way to remember the past.'' Jenny saw the soft light in Mrs. Buckwalter's eyes and envied the woman. The older woman didn't talk often about her late husband, but Jenny had wondered before if she thought of him. She frequently had that same half smile on her face when she seemed lost in thought.

"They're coming back!'' one of the teenage girls yelled from the hayloft. Several of the girls had climbed the steps up to the loft so they could watch the road from the small window there. "I see lights coming this way! And a horse!''

"Thank God,'' Mrs. Buckwalter said, all memories gone from her face. She turned to Jenny. "Can I help with the coffee, dear? Or anything else? My experience with crises is that they always make people hungry and thirsty.''

Jenny laughed. "I've got plenty of coffee. And there's enough of that cake left for another round.''

Mrs. Buckwalter was right. The ranch hands were the first ones through the door, their boisterous good humor relieving the last of the fears of the women inside.

"We got them. Everyone's back safe,'' one stocky man stopped to announce on his way to the refreshment table. "But it's colder than blazes out there. Hope there's some coffee left.''

Jenny started pouring coffee into the thick porcelain mugs that had been brought over from the restaurant. Thankfully the restaurant had been well stocked with dishes when the young engaged couple decided to reopen it this past Christmas. Linda and Duane, the couple, had volunteered the use of all the dishes for tonight's party and Jenny believed they would use every single one of them. There would be an enormous number of dishes to wash at some point and, as far as she could tell, there wasn't an automatic dishwasher anywhere around.

The barn door was opened and a damp cold filled the dance floor. Not that anyone was thinking about dancing. The music had stopped when the men left earlier and only the sound of muffled talking was heard now.

"The guy on the horse is bringing in the kidnappers," one short rancher offered to Jenny as he held his cup out to be filled. "He had some fancy moves, I don't mind telling you."

"The FBI agent?" Jenny was trying not to watch the door as it kept opening, but she couldn't help but notice that Robert wasn't back yet.

"Don't know what he is." The rancher picked up a stuffed mushroom as he held his cup in the other hand. "Didn't say nothing about who he was. Buckwalter seemed to know him, though. They made a fine team."

The rancher put the mushroom in his mouth.

"Glad it all worked out." Jenny wondered if they'd need more paper napkins.

The rancher didn't seem inclined to leave the refreshment table. He picked up a carved carrot piece and eyed Jenny shyly. "That fella Buckwalter—noticed you dancing with him. Are you—you know—"

Jenny looked up from the napkins.

"—you know, involved?"

"Mr. Buckwalter and me?"

The rancher beamed. "Guess not if you still call him Mister. I figured you weren't—what with all his money and everything. But wanted to be sure. Never held with moving in on another man's territory, not even when anyone could see the two of you are from different worlds. Guess you're free then."

Jenny started to protest, but the man didn't stop to draw a breath.

"My name's Chester, by the way. The boys call me Harry on account of Chest. You know, Chest, Hairy—"

"I'm sorry, but—"

"Not that there's any problem. With my chest, I mean. I got just the right amount of hair. You got nothing to worry about with me. I got me n-o-o defects. Just a regular kind of guy. That's me."

"I'm sure you're a fine man," Jenny moved a platter of toast squares to the back of the table. She'd take those over to the kitchen and make some new ones. She looked up at Chester. "But I'm too busy right now to visit."

"Maybe later?"

"There'll be cleanup later. Dishes."

The rancher looked dismayed. "I suppose I could help, even though with the touch of arthritis I get in my joints—well, I'm likely to be more trouble than good to you."

Jenny looked up and smiled. "I'll do fine with the dishes. Thanks anyway."

The barn door opened this time to a loud grumbling noise. A steady stream of frigid air blew into the barn making the pink streamers hanging from the beams start to sway.

The temperature in the room dropped ten degrees, but no one complained about the cold. Everyone was looking at the three unkempt men who reluctantly stomped into the barn, swearing as they were forced by their captors to come inside.

Jenny recognized two of the three men who were holding the shoulders of the prisoners. Garth Elkton was one. His top ranch hand was another. The third man, a stranger who obviously hadn't been to the dance because he wasn't in a suit, seemed to be in charge.

Jenny looked past all those men and saw nothing but the snow falling in the black night outside. The teenage boys had come inside minutes ago. The ranch hands all seemed to be back. Men and women were giving each other quick hugs of relief. A dusting of snow had settled on the walkway outside the barn and it was covered with a score or more of large boot prints. There were no other figures standing in the doorway waiting to come inside.

"That Buckwalter fella must be still parking the bus—if that's who you're looking for," the rancher who had stood at the table offered quietly. "He was the only one who knew how to drive the bus after the kids stripped the gears. Guess it's on account of him flying planes. We would have had to walk back if it weren't for him. He nursed the bus all the way back. He's not a bad guy for a rich man."

Then a final man appeared in the doorway and Jenny relaxed. Robert. I mean, she corrected herself, Mr. Buckwalter, was back safe. "No, he's not a bad guy."

"I wish you luck with him," the rancher offered quietly.

"Oh, no, I'm not—I mean there's no need—"

Just then Jenny heard the cell phone ring. The ring was faint and hard to hear over the talking of the ranchers and teenagers. She remembered Mrs. Buckwalter making a call so she assumed the older woman still had the phone and she was right.

"This is for you," Mrs. Buckwalter shouted to Jenny as she moved through the couples who were now brushing snow off of each other. The older woman was weaving between couples and getting closer to the refreshment table but she continued to yell, "Something about a pudding order that's late—"

Jenny winced. She was a full ten yards away from Robert. But she could hear his low chuckle over the murmured conversation of everyone else.

"Tell your sister hi," Robert called over to her. "And tell her I want a case of chocolate pudding with sprinkles if they have such a thing."

"Your sister sells pudding, dear?" Mrs. Buck-walter asked as she handed the phone to Jenny.

"She will be if she's not careful," Jenny said as she took the phone and stepped behind the refreshment table where it was quieter.

"I heard that," Jenny's sister said when Jenny put the phone to her ear. "And rest assured, I won't need to be looking for a new job. My boss is very happy with what I've discovered."

"And what would that be?" Jenny kept her voice low so that no one else could hear. Six or seven of the teenagers had drifted over to the refreshment table and were staring down at the punch bowl trying to decide whether or not to scoop some of the watered-down beverage into their plastic cups.

"Well, for starters, I know where Robert Buck-walter the Third is."

"Any number of people know that. It's not a secret."

"Well, none of the other tabloids know where he

is these days. And I know something's up. I told my boss that the man was very touchy about talking to the press.''

"He thought you were a pudding salesman, for Pete's sake. It had nothing to do with the press.''

"Still, I think he's hiding something. Some secret.''

"Well, if he is, it's his to keep. I, for one, am not going to ask him another thing about his life.''

"Oh, you've been talking to him?''

"No, I haven't been talking to him.''

"Oh.'' The disappointment in the voice of Jenny's sister was more personal than professional. She was suddenly Jenny's little sister again. "I'm sorry. I thought maybe after that kiss…''

Jenny couldn't help herself. She darted a quick look over her shoulder to be sure that no one was close enough to hear. "Well, he did ask me to dance.''

"You danced with him!'' Jenny's sister shrieked. "You danced with Robert Buckwalter the Third! Wait until I tell Mom! You really danced with him.''

"It was a short dance,'' Jenny was forced to admit. "The kidnapping sort of got everyone distracted.''

"Kidnapping! Somebody kidnapped him! Why didn't you say so! Now that's a newsbreak.''

"No, no, not Robert. It was someone else. He

didn't have anything to do with it. It's all tied up with some rustling that's going on."

"Oh." Jenny's sister paused. "Rustling? You mean for cows? You're sure the kidnappers weren't really out for him and they just grabbed the wrong person or something. I mean if you were going to kidnap anyone, he'd be the one to pick. He's got more money than the president of the United States. He certainly has more money than some cow."

"Yes, I'm sure. He wasn't the target."

Jenny sensed someone standing slightly behind her before she heard the man clear his throat. She looked up.

"Make sure she knows I didn't even know the kidnap victims," Robert said firmly. Snowflakes were melting on his hair and he still looked as if he'd stepped out of the pages of a catalog. "Make sure she knows the kidnapping had nothing to do with me. It would have happened if I hadn't been here."

"That's what I told her. I said you wouldn't have even gone with the men if it hadn't been for the bus. I mean your mother rented it and all."

"Well, I don't know about that." Robert frowned. How is it that he had never noticed Jenny's eyes turned a snapping black when she was annoyed? Fascinating. He wondered if she was annoyed with her sister or with him. Maybe she thought he should have ridden to the rescue on a horse like the FBI agent instead of worrying about a big old bus. He guessed a bus wasn't very dashing. If that was it, he needed to explain. "I would like to think I would go to anyone's aid if they were being kidnapped. It wasn't just the bus."

"What's this about some bus?" Jenny's sister asked on the phone. "Was it a school bus? Were there kids in danger? That would make a good angle."

"There is no angle. Robert—I mean, Mr. Buckwalter—was just driving."

Robert frowned deeper. He wasn't sure he liked the turn this conversation was taking. Granted, he didn't want his life splattered all over some tabloid in the morning, but he didn't know that he cared to have Jenny dismiss his efforts so lightly.

"It wasn't just easy driving," Robert finally said. "The gears had been stripped. I had to get everyone back here. It was cold enough out there to freeze to death if we didn't get back."

There, that should let her know his actions were important, he thought.

"What's that?" Jenny's sister spoke forcefully in Jenny's ear. "Put the receiver out more. I need to hear. I got the part about the kids in the school bus almost freezing to death. This is great. My boss will love this story."

"There is no story," Jenny said firmly.

"But what about the children?"

"There are no children."

"Well, then, what was the school bus doing? Work with me here, Jenny. It's not like this won't hit the local papers anyway. School bus kind of stuff always does. This is practically real news."

"Listen, to me—there are no children. There was no school bus."

"Well, then, give me a little something. Right this minute—what is Robert Buckwalter the Third doing?"

"He's just—" Jenny looked up at Robert. The snow had melted and his hair was wet now. His cheeks were still red and his nose was white. His hands shivered slightly as he held a cup of coffee in them. "He's just warming up."

"Ohhh, that's a good quote. Can I use that? Sources close to the man said that he is warming up and looking to be hot again."

"Absolutely not!"

"Well, then, can I talk to him? Ask him if I can do an interview."

"I'm sure he doesn't—"

"Just ask him. Please."

"Oh, all right." Jenny began as she put her hand over the receiver so her sister could not hear the conversation. "I know you won't want to—that's why I only said I'd ask. Not that you'd agree."

Robert watched the blush creep up Jenny's face

again. Her eyes had lightened again until he could see the caramel highlights in them.

"I'll do it," Robert said.

"But I haven't asked—"

"Oh."

"Not that you might not want to anyway. You might be able to sway the decision on the bachelor list and if that's what you want—"

"Did she give any hint of that?" Robert's face came to attention. "That she'd be willing to speak to the editors and plead my case?"

Robert wasn't sure that Jenny's sister could do anything to get him off that list, but if she was anything like Jenny he didn't want to underestimate her.

"I'll let you ask." Jenny held out the phone. She was defeated. Why try and protect the privacy of Robert Buckwalter when he obviously wanted people all across the country to read about him as they stood in line to buy groceries? She suddenly wished she had told her sister he was hot.

Robert took the phone from Jenny's hand.

A faint siren filtered into the barn and could be heard even over the commotion caused by the three kidnappers being tied up on the barn floor against their wishes.

"I want to negotiate," Robert said into the phone. "Agree to my terms and we'll talk."

Jenny looked up. "You have terms?"

Robert nodded emphatically to Jenny as he continued speaking into the phone. "That's right. I'll cooperate if you cooperate. And I assure you you'll get your story somehow." He listened and then grinned. "Yes, something with pictures. It might take me a day or two to work it out first. Talk to the editors. See what they say."

Jenny felt stiffer than she could remember feeling for years. Terms. He had terms. He was planning to sell his soul and become an underwear model.

Jenny almost missed the barn door opening once again. If it wasn't for the siren growing louder and then stopping, she wouldn't have paid much attention. But then she heard the booming voice of Sheriff Carl Wall.

"Where are they?" the sheriff demanded as he stomped into the room carrying two large suitcases.

"Careful with those." A platinum blonde stepped daintily behind him. "Those are alligator skin cases."

Jenny had never seen such a woman. Now there was somebody who could get away with modeling underwear. She was tall, thin and reeked of style. She was just a touch haughty and Jenny knew without a doubt that the hair color she wore was not her own.

The FBI agent seemed to share Jenny's suspicions that the woman was not one of the locals and he walked over to the woman. "I'll need to see some identification."

"Identification?" The woman stopped. She managed to look very offended. "I don't need any identification. I'm with him."

The woman pointed at Robert Buckwalter.

Jenny saw Robert flinch. He'd quietly pressed the off button on the cell phone, hanging up on her sister. That meant that whatever was going to be said now was something that Robert wanted to be kept from the press.

This is it, Jenny braced herself. That woman spells a secret if anyone does.

"Now, Laurel, you know that's not—"

The FBI agent appeared to have no patience. He looked at Robert. "She's with you?"

"I wouldn't say 'with'—I know Laurel, of course. Our families are, well… My mother knows her better—so, no, I wouldn't say 'with.'"

"It was 'with' enough for you on Christmas!" Laurel staged a pout that would have done justice to a Hollywood starlet.

Jenny nodded to herself. Of course.

"I didn't see you on Christmas!" Robert protested. It was colder than an Arctic winter inside this barn and he was starting to sweat. "I haven't seen you for months!"

"Well, maybe not this Christmas," Laurel agreed prettily. "You were a naughty boy and didn't come to my party. And here I'd counted on you."

Jenny started to breathe again. He hadn't seen her for months.

"I never said I would come," Robert said wearily.

He'd never said he would come. Jenny started to sing inside.

"Don't worry, I forgive you. I figure we have lots and lots of Christmases to spend together." Laurel stepped close and smiled at Robert confidently. "Laurel knows these things."

Jenny dropped the teaspoon she held in her hand. She wondered if Laurel did know these things. If the other woman did, she was ten steps ahead of Jenny who couldn't seem to figure out much about anything.

Chapter Six

"**B**ring those bags over here." Laurel looked behind her and spoke sharply to Sheriff Wall who was standing staring at Laurel. The sheriff looked down at his arms as though he'd forgotten they were attached to his shoulders let alone that they held two expensive bags.

Jenny looked around. The sheriff was not alone in his fascination with Laurel. The ranch hands had forgotten all about the hot coffee they'd been lining up to get. By the looks on their faces they no longer needed the coffee to warm them.

"I need my lipstick." Laurel pouted for the benefit of the men standing around. "My lips aren't used to weather like this." She shivered delicately. "Why, it's terrible out there."

Silence greeted her pronouncement.

"It is cold at that, ma'am," one of the ranch hands finally ventured to say.

Laurel smiled up at him. "You really should pick better weather for doing these cow things." She turned her head so her smile hit Robert. "What is it they called it—the rustle or something?"

"Rustling," Robert said dryly. "You're talking about the cattle rustling that has been going on around here. A hundred thousand dollars worth of loss so far. Interstate stuff. Enough to put some of these ranchers under. The FBI is working on the case now. It's serious here."

"Well, they need to plan it for a warmer time of year, don't you think?" She appealed to the sheriff who was bringing her bags to her. "Maybe you could talk to the people in charge of the rustling. Ask them to do it in the summer instead. We could have a lawn picnic then with umbrellas and iced tea."

"Yes, ma'am," Sheriff Wall replied automatically. He looked worried. "Where do you want me to set these bags?"

Laurel looked around, her eyes finally settling on the refreshment table.

Jenny winced. The refreshment table had looked better when the evening began. The teenagers had wrapped the legs in swirls of pink crepe paper and had twisted streamers from the table edge to the floor all along the front of the table. But those streamers were gone now, leaving stubby pieces of tape behind. And the lace tablecloth borrowed from Mrs. Hargrove had a half-dozen brown circles where some coffee cup had spilled. The punch bowl still stood in the center, even though only an inch or two of liquid remained in its bottom.

"I can't put my bags there," Laurel appealed to Robert. "They're genuine alligator. They'll get wet with that stuff." She pointed to the punch bowl.

"If they're alligator, I expect they'll be fine if they get wet." Robert shook his head. He added in disgust, "The skin's been wet before when it was on the alligator. I can't believe you'd buy alligator skin luggage anyway. Aren't they some kind of endangered group or something?"

The other men were more forgiving and more eager to please. One of the ranch hands took off his vest and laid it over the tablecloth. "Here. I think your bags are beautiful. And don't worry. You can put your bags on this. Won't hurt my old vest any."

"Why, aren't you kind?" Laurel gushed at the man and then looked over at the sheriff. "You can put them there."

The sheriff set the bags on top of the vest and then ducked his head, mumbling something about getting back to the kidnappers.

"Kidnappers?" Laurel looked up with the first genuine expression that Jenny had seen on the woman's face yet. Laurel's smile was gone and she looked twenty percent smarter. "I thought you said they were cattle rustlers."

"Well, they're also kidnappers," the sheriff said somewhat sourly.

"Oh, dear, I knew I shouldn't have come here to this end-of-the-world place where there aren't even police to protect me from the criminals that run loose."

"I'm the law around here." The sheriff stomped a little louder than he needed to on his way over to the tangle of kidnappers that were waiting for him on the floor. "I protect all the citizens of Dry Creek." He smiled up at Laurel. "And the visitors, too, of course. I take good care of visitors."

"But there's only one of you." Laurel looked aghast just thinking about it. "The Seattle police force must have thousands of people working. And they're trained. Police academy and all that."

"I've got my GED. I know it's not the same as a high school diploma, but I know the same information. And I read those police magazines every month. And not just the free ones they send. Sometimes I buy the ones off the shelves at that big drugstore in Billings. Just don't go listening to anyone spouting off about that hit man that came here after Miss Glory. There was no way I could have known he'd dress up like Santa Claus and come to the church pageant just like he belonged—"

"Hitman! You had a hit man, too. Right here in

Dry Creek!'' Laurel fanned her cheeks with one hand. ''A girl like me just isn't safe.''

''No one can get into Dry Creek that easily,'' Robert said, trying to stem her rising hysteria. When he said it, he looked at Laurel more closely. It was true. Dry Creek wasn't the easiest place to get to in the middle of a February blizzard. What had prompted Laurel to come?

''I'm sure we're all safe,'' Jenny added. She was standing behind the refreshment table still pouring coffee. The line of men wanting a cup was finally moving forward. The heat from the coffee urn had added a moist flush to Jenny's face and she was beginning to wish she had her hair net back so that her hair would stay in place.

Laurel turned to Jenny and scrutinized her briefly before dismissing her. ''Well, I'm sure you're perfectly safe, dear. But rich people have extra perils and anyone can see I have money.''

''What anyone can see—'' Robert interrupted icily ''—is that you don't have the manners you were born with. Look around you. Money isn't the measure of a person. Some of these people will never have an extra dime and they're still better people that you or I will ever be with our silver spoons and our trust funds.''

One of two of the ranch hands looked at Robert in appreciation.

''Say what you want.'' Laurel stepped over and

snapped open one of her small alligator suitcases. "But I've never heard of anyone pulling a gun on someone else because they wanted to steal from a better kind of person. They're after people with money and that's it."

Laurel lifted the lid on her suitcase and a wave of perfume hit the air.

The man holding his coffee cup out to Jenny strained to see over her shoulder so Jenny turned to see what the attraction was. There she saw it. Row after folded row of satin and silk lingerie. Some trimmed with lace. Some appliquéd. Slips. Nighties. In peach. Ivory. Lavender. White.

"And you're worried about the kids becoming underwear salesmen," Robert said quietly as he moved closer to Jenny. "I'd say she's set up for a sales tour of all fifty states."

The amused tone in Robert's voice cheered Jenny up considerably. He might be rich. But he surely could still see through a woman like Laurel.

"Didn't you pack any real clothes?" Robert finally asked. "You certainly can't survive a blizzard with that kind of stuff. You need long johns and sweaters with maybe some sweatpants and wool scarves."

"Oh, I had two other boxes of clothes, but they got lost in the airport baggage system somewhere. I expect they're at the Billings airport by now. Anyway, they're going to send them out when they can," Laurel answered cheerfully. "Not that they have any of those blizzard clothes in them. I brought some special-occasion clothes instead."

Laurel looked at Robert with a glance he could only call sweetly possessive. It made him nervous. He'd known Laurel for years. They'd actually gone to school together, so he was better prepared for her games than most. He knew the sweetness was an act. He just didn't know why she was playing up to him. "There are no special occasions planned here."

"We'll see." Laurel smiled smugly.

Laurel shut the lid on her suitcase and swung around a little designer purse. "You know, I think the lipstick is still in my purse. Silly me. I didn't need to rummage around in that suitcase after all."

Laurel pulled a long gold lipstick tube out of her purse along with a small mirror. She looked over at the men. "I don't suppose one of you would hold this mirror up for me, would you? I just don't feel right unless my lipstick is fresh."

The request almost caused a fight among the ranch hands until Laurel turned and asked. "Robert, would you help me?"

Robert grimaced. Yes, this was Laurel at her best. What could he do? If he didn't hold the mirror, a half dozen of those ranch hands would go home tonight with black eyes. And the punch bowl might get broken. He happened to know the bowl was a favorite of Mrs. Hargrove's.

"Why don't you prop the mirror up on that ledge over there?" Robert pointed. The barn, even though it was now a community center, had been built for working cattle and still showed the marks. "See, you can see where the stall used to be?"

Laurel gasped. "You expect me to use the remains of a cow stall!"

"Well, there hasn't been a cow along that wall in ten years. I don't see the harm."

Laurel tried to contain her annoyance, but it showed. Her normally pink cheeks got a little redder. Her baby blue eyes narrowed. Her chin jutted out in a stubborn angle. Then she took a deep breath and smiled sweetly back at Robert. "You're right, you know."

Laurel turned to walk over to the ledge and Robert watched her. She was definitely up to something.

"Anyone else want coffee?" Jenny asked the men standing around the table. They were blocking the way for the other people who wanted something to drink by standing there and watching the blonde.

"I'll take another cup," one ranch hand said with a sigh. "She's way out of my league anyway."

"Well, of course she is, Kingman," another ranch hand responded as he got back in line, too. "She's way too pretty for any of us. But we can still look.

She's like a picture in one of those fancy magazines."

"Yes, she is," Jenny agreed. She knew how the ranch hands felt. Sometimes you couldn't help being drawn to someone even though you knew you didn't have a chance in a million of anything happening.

"She shouldn't have come here," Robert said as he looked over the people of Dry Creek. Some ranch hands were still drooling over Laurel as she dramatically rubbed her lipstick on repeatedly. He'd lay odds there'd be some sharp words exchanged among those boys before the night was over. The teenage boys weren't far behind the ranch hands and the girls were looking like they were ready to mutiny. Even the married farm couples looked uneasy. "Laurel doesn't belong in a place like this."

Jenny lifted her chin. She'd emptied the coffeepot and the line had ended. "There's nothing wrong with this place."

"I didn't mean—" Robert was brought back sharply. "Of course, there's nothing wrong with this place. It's a great place full of great people."

"Just because it used to be a cow barn doesn't mean it's any less of a place," Jenny continued like he hadn't even spoken. "It's a place filled with friendship and good people—well except for them maybe." She nodded her chin at the kidnappers who were now neatly tied at one side of the barn. "And who knows—even they might not be so very bad when all is said and done.''

''I agree.'' Robert moved closer to stand beside Jenny. He didn't know how to say what he was thinking. ''I like the people here. I like that this used to be a cow barn.''

''It's because you're slumming, isn't it?'' Jenny said quietly. The punch bowl was now empty so she pulled the ladle out. ''Getting a dose of real life before you settle down in some mansion somewhere with a perfect wife and perfect kids.''

''That's not it at all.''

Jenny had a sudden fierce wish to have her hair net back. She knew now why she was always so insistent on wearing it even in food situations where the health code didn't require one. It reminded her of who she was in the situation. She was the chef. She knew her place. She wasn't a guest.

''Excuse me.'' Jenny forced a smile. ''I better start cleaning up or I'll be here all night.''

''Well, you're not going to clean up alone,'' Robert protested. ''Tell me what to do and where to start.''

''You can't help—not in that tuxedo. You'll ruin it.''

''I don't care about the tuxedo.''

''It's wasteful to ruin a ten-thousand dollar suit doing dishes.'' Jenny felt her jaw set. If she needed any reminding about the difference between herself and Robert Buckwalter, this was certainly it. He could ruin an Italian tuxedo just because he wanted to do something else at that point in time.

Robert looked down at the suit. It probably had cost over ten thousand dollars. But who needed a suit like this, for goodness' sake? He'd just never given any thought before to how much he spent on clothes.

"Even taking in the punch bowl won't work. It's sticky with sugar and almost impossible to carry without holding it against yourself," Jenny said as she reached for the bowl herself. "What you could do is gather up the coffee cups while I take the bowl to the café and rinse it out."

"You can't go outside alone."

"Why not? The kidnappers are caught."

"These guys are caught. There could be more out there."

Jenny looked up. Someone had put another slow song on the record player. But no one was dancing. She could tell that the party was winding down. "I think with all these people here they would have spotted a stranger."

"They didn't spot Santa Claus when he was the hit man and almost got that woman—the one they called Dry Creek's angel," he protested. "Besides, I'd prefer to come with you."

Jenny shrugged as she put on a jacket Mrs. Hargrove had lent her for the evening. "It's just across the parking lot."

"You need someone to open the doors anyway."

Robert followed Jenny to the barn door. The sheriff and some of the other men were squatted down on the floor in one corner talking to the kidnappers.

"Think they're the last of the lot?" Robert asked the men as he stood by the door.

The sheriff nodded. The man looked a lot more competent dealing with the kidnappers than when handling Laurel and her luggage. "I'm sure we're safe for now anyway. He—" the sheriff jerked his head at the FBI agent "—thinks someone in Dry Creek is an inside informant on this rustling business, but even if that's true we should be safe tonight."

Robert nodded his thanks as he opened the door for Jenny.

The stars were no longer showing in the night sky and flakes of snow steadily blew in from the north. The men had stomped down much of the snow earlier but the boot prints were filling with the latest batch of snow.

"I doubt half these cars will start," Robert said as he looked at the twenty-some odd vehicles parked around the barn.

Robert had never felt cold like this before. He'd given his coat to the old man earlier and had insisted the man keep it. Now he was glad one of the ranch hands had pressed a wool jacket into his hands as Robert was heading out. Even with the jacket, his heart pounded faster to keep warm. He'd swear his eyelids were freezing.

"They've got jumper cables," Jenny said through chattering teeth.

A dim light was on in the café's porch and Robert opened the porch door quickly. Even though the porch was boarded together and the wind blew in through some of the holes, it was several degrees warmer inside.

"Let me get the door," Robert said as he reached for the main door. "Do you have a key?"

"It's not locked. They left it open for us tonight."

"Then you better let me check it out first. Someone could have come inside."

In the yellow light of the porch, Jenny could see her breath come out in white puffs. Her lips were stiff from the cold and she felt snowflakes melting in her hair.

"But what would you do anyway if someone was in there? You don't have a weapon."

"Well, neither one of us has a weapon."

"I have this bowl."

"You wouldn't dare break Mrs. Hargrove's bowl over someone's head. From what I hear, that bowl has served the punch for every wedding in this community for the past forty years. It's practically a tradition all by itself."

"It is a nice bowl. Heavier than it looks, too. Real cut glass."

Robert had bent low and was looking in the glass panes of the café door. It looked like the only upright shadows inside were from chairs although it was hard to tell because the girls had used the café as a changing room and there were T-shirts and jeans everywhere. "I'm going in. Give it a minute and then follow."

The doorknob was as cold as any metal Robert had ever gripped. But it turned easily and he stepped into the café. The air inside still smelled of cooking. He thought it was the stuffed mushrooms he smelled.

Robert flipped on the overhead light for the café and saw that the jumble looked undisturbed from the last time he had walked through. "Let me check out the kitchen first before you come in."

Without waiting for an answer, Robert walked toward the back of the room where the kitchen door was. The café was small so he reached the other side with a few strides. The light in the kitchen revealed all was safe there, as well.

Robert heard the cell phone ring on the porch. It must still be in Jenny's apron pocket. He'd bet a punch bowl full of pudding that it was Jenny's sister calling. Which reminded him, he owed her a story. Assuming, of course, that she was able to get him off that cursed list.

"For you," Jenny called as she walked across the café and into the kitchen. "It's my sister."

Jenny listened as Robert and her sister talked. Robert paced as he walked. Up and down the cold kitchen. His cheeks were red from the temperature and his dark hair was wet where snow had melted now that he was in the relative warmth of the kitchen. He looked excited though, wheeling and dealing with her sister. He said goodbye with laughter.

"Your sister is something," Robert reported as he hung up the phone. "Those editors will have their hands full with her."

"She is, isn't she?"

The outside door to the café opened and Jenny and Robert both stiffened until they heard Mrs. Hargrove. "I hope you're not doing dishes at this time of night."

The kitchen door opened and the older woman stood there with a wool scarf wrapped around her head and a blanket thrown over her shoulders like a shawl. "We've had so much excitement tonight, the dishes need to wait. Tomorrow's Saturday. Enough snow is predicted to close all the roads. We'll have nothing better to do than dishes. I've already asked Mr. Gossett to help us. It'll help settle him down. He's been anxious lately."

"But if the roads are closed, we won't be able to get to the café from Garth's ranch," Jenny said.

"And I can't leave the two of you with all these dishes."

"I've got extra rooms at my house. You're both welcome to spend the night at my place."

"Robert doesn't need to—" Jenny began in alarm. A man like him shouldn't be helping with cleanup.

"I'd be delighted." Robert accepted the older woman's invitation.

Robert grinned. Things were working out better than he could have hoped. He'd have some talking time with Jenny tonight and tomorrow.

"I already invited your friend—" Mrs. Hargrove smiled at Robert.

Robert's grin froze.

"—or fiancée, I guess I should say. Considering that she brought a wedding dress with her to Dry Creek."

"She brought a what!"

Chapter Seven

"Now, Laurel, you take the room at the top of the stairs and to your left. That's next to mine. Robert, you'll have the couch in the living room. And Jenny, the room down that hall has a bed in it already made up. That room is closest to the furnace and should be toasty." Mrs. Hargrove smiled at Jenny. "It's my sewing room and the bed in there is my best. You'll need a good night's sleep after all you've done today, dear. Such a wonderful dinner party."

"Thank you," Jenny whispered. She could have slept under a cardboard box in some old alley. A sewing room would be heaven. She was damp, cold and tired. She just wanted the day to end. She didn't know whether or not she believed Robert's vehement protests that he wasn't engaged to be married to anyone, but she did know she was ready to be alone. She'd been right not to trust a rich man with any tiny bit of her heart.

The walk across the snow to Mrs. Hargrove's house hadn't been long, but Jenny felt like it had taken an eternity. She didn't have snow boots so she had to follow in the footsteps Mrs. Hargrove made. But it wasn't just the snow that seeped into her shoes that made her cold and tired.

It was all of *this*. She glared at Robert. She just wasn't cut out for this—the kind of roller-coaster life that people like Robert and Laurel seemed to lead. Jenny was a simple person and liked to deal with people who were straightforward—people you could trust to be who they said they were. Not something like this.

Who really knew who was engaged to who? It was like the dating game with extra doors for people to pop in and out of whenever they took a fancy to do so.

The bottom line was that Laurel said she had a wedding dress sitting in a box at the Billings airport. That was part of the special-occasion clothes she'd talked about earlier. The sheriff hadn't had room to bring the box to Dry Creek in his patrol car. But there it was—waiting in Billings.

No woman traveled around with a wedding dress unless she had a reason. And if Robert Buckwalter III was getting a visit from a woman who was so sure of herself that she brought a wedding dress along, why was he kissing another woman? Especially when the kiss was a whopper of a kiss like the one Jenny had gotten from him.

Not that any kiss meant anything to a man like Robert, Jenny took a deep breath and reminded herself. She knew the rich kissed everyone, from their hairdressers to their dog trainers. A kiss from a rich man meant nothing. Absolutely nothing. A handshake was probably more sincere.

Robert watched Jenny walk down the hall. Her back was military straight. He knew she hadn't believed him about Laurel even though he'd said everything he could to convince her he wasn't secretly engaged to Laurel or anyone else. He certainly didn't know anything about a wedding dress!

To make it worse, Jenny wouldn't come right out and say she didn't believe him. She just kept repeating that it was none of her business and it didn't matter whom he married or what kind of a dress the woman wore.

Robert knew there was a world of difference between "I believe you" and "it doesn't matter." Especially when Jenny had pulled that hair net of hers back on like it was armor.

"You run along, dear." Mrs. Hargrove smiled at Laurel who had allowed herself to be coaxed into accepting Mrs. Hargrove's invitation when it was apparent there was no hotel around. "I want Robert

to help me bring in some wood before we all bed
down. We won't be long.''

Laurel could have helped Robert out of his dilemma, but she wouldn't. She kept a bored smile on
her face that revealed little.

Once Laurel made her bombshell announcement
she apparently felt free to ignore him. Which would
have been a dead giveaway about the true nature of
their acquaintance if it wasn't for the pouty face that
Laurel put on for the show. She looked enough like
a woman who'd been wronged to turn others to her
defense.

Robert sighed. His protests fell on skeptical ears.
The truth was he hadn't even been around Laurel
for months. They had moved in the same social circle for years, but he had long ago made it a policy
to spend as little time alone with her as possible.

Even though the cold outside had iced every inch
of tree and shrub, Robert was glad to be able to go
out of the house and gather wood for the fire.

Mrs. Hargrove had a stack of logs neatly arranged
in a small shed on the south side of her house. Robert had offered to get the logs by himself, but Mrs.
Hargrove had politely insisted on coming with him.

He found out why when he had his arms half-full
of frozen pine logs.

''I run a godly household,'' the older woman said.
She had a plaid wool scarf wrapped around her chin,
but her words still came out clear. ''It's late so I'll

come to the point—everyone sleeps in their own bed."

"Of course."

The woman nodded in satisfaction. "Just wanted to be sure we understood each other. I don't know who you're engaged to—"

"I'm not engaged to anyone."

Mrs. Hargrove pinned him with her eyes. "You've got one woman who says you are. Why would she be saying that if it's not true?"

"I don't know for sure." Robert added another log to the stack in his arms. "But my guess would be that she's trying to get her name in the paper."

Robert had been asking himself that same question for the past half hour and the only reason he could think of was that Laurel had somehow found out about the bachelor list.

He'd suspected before that Laurel funneled information about him to the tabloids. That was one of the reasons he'd started avoiding her. But she could still get information about him from other people in their social set and pass it along. If that was what she was doing, it would appear that the communication flowed in both directions.

Someone must have told Laurel he was a candidate for the big slot on the tabloid's list. Laurel loved the spotlight. She'd see it as quite a triumph to announce her engagement to the number one bachelor in the U.S. at the same time, or shortly after he was named the most eligible bachelor around. The fact that Robert would deny the engagement the next day wouldn't matter. Her picture would already be in every tabloid from here to Japan before Robert could get it all sorted out. Laurel would soak up the publicity. She might even get a book deal out of it.

Mrs. Hargrove looked perplexed. "She'd get engaged just to get her name in the paper? They put the names of the bridal couples in the *Billings Gazette*, too, but I've never heard of anyone getting married just to see their name there."

"It wouldn't be the *Billings Gazette*." Robert wished that that's all his marriage would ever mean to the media—just a nice paragraph in the Newly Married column of the local paper. "I'm trying to get out of it, but some New York paper has got me picked for number one in some one hundred best bachelor list they're doing. When the list hits the newsstands, it will be all across the country. There'll be pictures. My credit rating will rise. Companies will call me to be their spokesman. I'll be offered free cruises—free everything."

"Free cruises! My goodness! Well, congratulations!" Mrs. Hargrove beamed briefly until she looked at his face. She continued more carefully. "That's quite an honor to be number one. And a free cruise—I can't imagine—I've never even been to Seattle. And a cruise! I think that's exciting—to actually be on the ocean. But you don't look very happy about it. I can't imagine why you want out of the list if it has a free cruise with it.''

"It's not just any free cruise. It's more like a free cruise on the *Titanic*."

"Well, still, being number one—that's got to be some kind of an accomplishment to take pride in.''

Robert snorted. "Being number one is like being tagged Public Property Number One. You're nothing but an object for the curious. Men hate you. Women hunt you. Literally. They won't let you go. They want to know everything from your shoe size to the kind of grades you got in junior high school. It's like they want to be your best friend without even meeting you. And most of them don't want to meet you. The kind of crowd we're talking about here just wants to be seen with you.''

Mrs. Hargrove was silent for a moment. "Let me make you a cup of tea and we'll sit and talk if you'd like. Seems to me you've got yourself in quite a fix.''

Robert looked up. "I'd like the tea, but I don't mean to worry anyone. I've been listed before. Not this big, but if I can't get out of it I'll still survive.''

"Oh, it's not just the list. You can deal with that. It's the rest of your life I'm worried about. You need to know what kind of a life that will be. You haven't begun to understand the important questions in life.'' The older woman picked up a couple of logs of her own. "Even with the cruises and everything, I'm sure being a rich man can't be easy."

Robert snorted again. "Being rich is the least of my worries."

"That's good, because I don't know anything about being rich. I'm doing good just to understand the troubles of a poor person." Mrs. Hargrove stepped up the snow-packed stairs to her front door. She looked down at Robert who stood on the walk below her. "But I do know this—and I know it because I've got the best instruction book for life ever put down on paper—being rich can be dangerous to the soul. The rich need to be pitied sometimes. They used to say a rich man had a harder time getting into heaven than a camel had going through the eye of a needle."

Robert was startled. No one had ever pitied him. Ever. Especially not for having money.

Mrs. Hargrove turned the knob on her door and opened it. "Always did think it was strange to compare a rich man to a camel. I saw a camel on one of those nature shows on television once. It was an ugly beast."

"And they spit," Robert added as he stepped behind her into the house. He wasn't sure how he felt about being pitied. For starters, it made him cranky. And being compared to a camel? "Smelly, stubborn animals with the personality of a cardboard box. The only reason anyone tolerates them is because they store all the water inside those humps of theirs and people need them to get around.''

Just like me, Robert realized with a start. I store a great deal of money and people need me and my money to get around.

Robert was back at the same place he had been earlier in the evening when he was talking to the minister. He knew people tolerated him—well, more than tolerated, they usually fawned all over him— because he could write big checks to support their favorite projects. Presto—be nice to Robert and he could make things happen. All kinds of things. Important things. Even silly things.

Right now, if he wanted, he could fly in a team of real camels to meet Mrs. Hargrove. He could even pay the best Hollywood stylists to come and give them such glamorous makeovers that Mrs. Hargrove would change her mind about their camel looks.

All it took was money.

And he had money. A depressing amount of cold hard cash.

But, Robert admitted finally, in the end it was only money, And money was a poor lover of the heart.

The trouble with money was that it clouded the issue. Everyone loved him when he had money. But who would still love him if he were poor and ugly as a desert camel? There was his mother, of course.

But his circle of friends dwindled dramatically at the thought of poverty. Robert had too many friends like Laurel. Lightweight friends at best.

He had made more true friends in his five months as Bob than he had made in a lifetime as Robert.

Maybe—the thought came in a whisper—maybe because Robert had always relied on his money to make him his friends.

Robert, he was afraid, was a lazy friend.

Oh, Robert was good at attracting women and he was good at writing checks to charity, but was he good at loving anyone?

Robert didn't want to admit it, but he was suddenly unsure. He didn't even have a pet. No one depended on him and he let no one down. That rooster Charlie was the closest thing he'd ever had to a dependent—and Charlie didn't rely on Robert for anything more than the rooster's handful of morning grain.

"Of course, you might think you already know everything there is to know about life and love," Mrs. Hargrove said softly. "A lot of young people do, you know."

"I can't speak for other people," Robert said. "But when it comes to me, I don't know any more about love than a desert camel knows about swimming the English Channel. I'd be grateful if you'd help me learn a thing or two about it before I drown in my own misery."

Mrs. Hargrove started to unwind her wool scarf. "That's the spirit. Let's get ready. We've got work to do."

The morning crept up on Robert as he lay on the living room couch. Teacups sat in the kitchen sink. He had dozed throughout the night without going to sleep deeply. Mrs. Hargrove had given him one of the Bibles she gave to the kids in her Sunday school class. The book, just the New Testament and some of the Psalms, had a picture of Jesus on the cover, with his arm stretched out to children. Some blue sea was in the background and the children all had perfect teeth.

Robert had read snatches of the book throughout the night. The words were simple enough so that a child could understand. By morning, Robert's mind was reeling from the freshness of his encounter.

Robert had gone to church services a few times in his life before, but this—this reading was intimate and disturbing. He knew in his bones that God was there with him. It was eerie and comforting all at the same time.

Still, he'd rather God had some flesh on Him. It would be easier to talk to Him face-to-face. And then maybe not, Robert thought. He wasn't ready for God to look him in the eye.

Robert's first thought was how unprepared he was. Mrs. Hargrove was right. He, Robert, didn't have a clue about how to love anyone, including God. However, if he learned one thing by reading the New Testament, it was that God helped those who came to Him and asked for help in learning to love both other people and Himself.

He also learned that there was no time like right now to begin.

Robert decided he'd practice by loving those around him. He'd start with Mrs. Hargrove.

"It's for a cruise," Robert announced when Mrs. Hargrove came downstairs and looked at the check he'd placed on the coffee table. "I'd thought about buying an ocean liner, but I knew you'd rather just go with other people. Maybe that man I saw you dancing with last night."

Mrs. Hargrove was in curlers and a fuzzy robe. The morning light was still thin but Robert was fully dressed in the tuxedo from last night. He felt good.

"That's Doris June's father! He's here visiting from Anchorage. Works for some television station there—KTCB or something. Last night, Doris June was dancing with some of the ranch hands. But she hated to leave her father sitting there alone so I helped out. I was only being friendly." Mrs. Hargrove looked at the check on the table like it was a coiled snake. "I couldn't just go off on a cruise with some television man from Alaska."

"There's enough money for separate cabins,"

Robert explained quickly. "I know you like everyone sleeping in their own bed."

"Still, I don't know him. I mean, of course, I
know him. He's a very pleasant man and—in other
circumstances—I mean, to dinner maybe. I'd even
hoped—" Mrs. Hargrove blushed. "Maybe a
movie. He'd mentioned driving into Miles City for
a movie. But a cruise! Why, what would he think
of me?"

"You don't have to go." Robert backtracked fast.
"Or you can take a woman friend if you'd like. The
only reason I thought of a man was the dancing."

Mrs. Hargrove had picked the check up and was
squinting at it with more interest now. "That's a
check for twenty thousand dollars."

Robert nodded, satisfied. It wasn't even breakfast
yet and he'd already got one down on the love situation. Pretty good, if he did say so himself.

Mrs. Hargrove grunted and then neatly tore the
check in half.

"What are you doing? That's twenty thousand
dollars!" He happened to know that Mrs. Hargrove
was living on her Social Security check. She could
use twenty thousand dollars.

"It's not about money." She tore the check into
quarters.

"It is when it's twenty thousand dollars you just
threw away! You could have taken a cruise around
the world."

Mrs. Hargrove looked over at the sofa. The child's Bible was still lying facedown on the arm of the sofa. "I've dealt with children and their bribes before. Of course, theirs is usually some kind of candy or sometimes flowers. But for now, no presents for me. I'd rather have you recite me a verse of the Scriptures. What did you learn last night?"

"That check was solid, you know."

Mrs. Hargrove smiled. "I never doubted that. What I want to know is if you're as solid as your check—with God, I mean."

"I'm going to learn how to love Him."

"Good."

"I don't know how yet. I thought I'd start with people first."

"Keep reading that." She nodded to the Bible. "And you'll learn all about loving God and loving other people."

"Yes, ma'am. I was hoping you might give me some advice. I'm sort of in need of some quick fixes here." Robert nodded down the hall toward Jenny's door. He'd thought about her last night, too.

"Don't write a check. If you want to love someone, do it from your heart. Put yourself in their place and listen to what they want. That goes for other people and for God. Of course, God has always made it pretty clear what He wants from people."

"I know there's the ten percent thing," Robert said. He'd always been a generous person. He believed in giving his money away before the rust got to it. Of course, rust didn't grow that fast and no one had ever expected that big of a cut before. Robert took a deep breath. It was a lot, but he was willing to give it. He hadn't expected a new life to come cheap. "That's pretty steep, but I plan to speak to my accountant first thing Monday morning. It'll take some calculating, but we'll do it."

"It won't be enough."

"Ten percent's my limit."

"Not enough. It's worthless."

"Worthless!" Robert looked at the scraps of check that the older woman still held in her hands. Maybe her hair curlers were screwed on too tight. "You do know that check was good, don't you? I have a bank balance that would probably shock you."

"Your bank balance will never be enough."

Robert looked over at her. "It's pretty impressive."

Mrs. Hargrove smiled sweetly. "No, it isn't. God doesn't want your money. What God wants is you. You are all you've got to give to Him that matters."

Robert was speechless for a moment. He wasn't sure Mrs. Hargrove had conferred with the man upstairs on this one. "I think maybe I'll still talk to my accountant on Monday about that ten percent check."

"I wouldn't just yet, dear. Trust me. God wants much more than your money. He wants your heart."

Mrs. Hargrove's words stayed in Robert's mind until they sat at the kitchen table and the oatmeal was served. He'd talked a good game to himself earlier, but Robert never really expected anyone— not even the supreme ruler of the universe—to refuse a Buckwalter check. Robert's world was turned upside down and he didn't quite know how to walk yet.

It didn't help that both Laurel and Jenny sat at the table beside him.

Saturday breakfast was at eight o'clock, Mrs. Hargrove informed all three of them cheerfully as she passed a plate of wheat toast. She'd made an exception this morning and allowed everyone to sleep in until nine.

"With all the excitement last night, I knew you'd need some extra sleep," the older woman said. "It was quite the party."

Jenny nodded and accepted a piece of toast. "I'll always remember those kids dancing away. I haven't seen a group of kids enjoy themselves so much for a long time."

"You like dancing, then?" Robert asked. He hadn't thought Jenny was a fanatic about dancing, but if she was she'd be easy to please.

Give me a break on this one, Father, Robert said inside and then almost jumped. He'd never thought about doing that kind of praying before. His only other prayers had been spoken at public functions as a way of thanking some nonspecific deity for the overcooked chicken and peas. He could as well have been praying to the chicken for all the difference it made anywhere. But this inside praying was like handling electrical wires. He could feel the current ready to move.

"Not particularly," Jenny said suspiciously as she passed the plate of toast on to Laurel. "I dance some, but not often."

Robert smiled at Jenny. He tried to make it a reassuring smile. Grandfatherly. But he could tell from the blush that started climbing her neck that he only succeeded in looking like an old leech. His smile widened to a full grin. He loved Jenny in pink. She'd even worn that old hair net of hers to breakfast, but he didn't care. He knew he was getting to her. She wouldn't blush up like this otherwise.

Jenny looked over at Laurel. "Toast?"

"I prefer rye," Laurel said as she made no attempt to reach for the plate.

Robert winced. He hoped he'd never been that dense.

"Mrs. Hargrove has wheat toast this morning," Robert said as pleasantly as he could. "Maybe you'd like a bowl of oatmeal instead."

Laurel looked at him like he'd suggested she suck on a raw egg. "I'm on a regime of food. It's the latest thing at Benji's.'' Robert recognized the famous Hollywood spa. "Everyone's doing it since Liz had such good success. But the items I must eat are very specific.'' Laurel looked over at Mrs. Hargrove and smiled slightly. "I'm sure you don't mind.''

"Of course not,'' Mrs. Hargrove said as she accepted the toast plate back and set it on the table. "But wheat bread is all I have.''

"But surely, I can get…'' Laurel's voice trailed off as her alarm grew. She drew herself together and gracefully conceded. "I guess the toast would do if I could have some freshly squeezed wheatgrass to go with it.''

Robert closed his eyes. He was sure God didn't intend for him to show any brotherly love to a ninny like Laurel. Still.

"There's three feet of snow out front,'' Robert said mildly. Patiently, he thought. "No one's going shopping today.''

"But my regime—''

"Will have to wait,'' Robert finished for her. "There's not a blade of fresh wheatgrass for miles around anyway. If there had been one that FBI agent's horse would have eaten it by now.''

Robert thought he'd been pleasant. A monk filled with brotherly patience couldn't have done better.

The pink left Jenny's face and her chin went up.

Then Jenny looked at him like he'd been deliberately rude to a kitten.

"Some people—like your fiancée—have health concerns," Jenny said. "You might be more understanding and not compare her diet to a horse's."

Laurel gave a horrified choking sound. "Horses eat that?"

Robert turned to Jenny.

"She's not my fiancée and I didn't say she eats with horses. I understand wheatgrass is healthy." He didn't even say he knew it wasn't health that was on Laurel's mind. It was social standing. "By tomorrow, who knows, maybe there's grass at some store in Miles City. We'll be able to go for supplies and check it out."

"I doubt it," Mrs. Hargrove said cheerfully as she stood up and turned to go get the coffeepot. "The snowplow won't get all the roads plowed today. They need to come over from Miles City. Usually takes a day or two. Maybe three."

"Three days!" Jenny looked horrified. "But we need to get supplies before then."

"Do you have a regime, too?" Laurel asked. It was the first time since she'd come into the barn last night that she looked genuinely interested in anyone but herself.

"No, but those kids. They'll drive me crazy if I feed them macaroni and cheese again. I'd planned on going shopping today, or tomorrow at the latest."

"What do you need?" Robert sensed an answer to prayer. He could give Jenny something she wanted. *Good work, Father.*

"Ten dozen taco shells and some hamburger would be a good start. Some pizza dough mix and some pepperoni. And some fresh romaine lettuce with vine-ripened tomatoes."

"Romaine lettuce? That doesn't sound like the kids," Robert said. He'd taken out a check and was writing the list on the back of it. He caught Mrs. Hargrove's eyes and deliberately turned the check over and quickly wrote "VOID" so she'd know the check was only a piece of notepaper to him at the moment. She smiled her approval.

"Oh, the kids don't like romaine. The salad's for me." Jenny smiled like she was remembering a special meal. "Just for me."

Bingo, Father. "I'll get you some."

"Don't be ridiculous," Jenny said. She spooned up some oatmeal. "In case you haven't noticed, the only store around is the hardware store. Trust me, they don't have any lettuce of any kind." Jenny suddenly remembered that farm animals sometimes eat vegetables—all that talk about horses and wheatgrass. Maybe there was hope. She looked over at Mrs. Hargrove. "They don't, do they? Maybe there's some special horse stuff. Really, any kind of greens would do. Like celery or something like carrots. I know horses like carrots."

Mrs. Hargrove shook her head. "Nobody has any fresh produce of their own, either. No gardens this time of year. Old man Gossett used to have some wild celery in that area behind his house, but that's buried under a foot of snow. Besides, I'm not too sure it's not poisonous. Tried to get him to dig it up, but he's a stubborn old fool."

Robert looked at Jenny. "Anything else you want?" Like maybe a small island or a diamond ring.

"Black pepper. We're running low on black pepper."

Robert wrote it down. He had his list and he had a plan.

Chapter Eight

Steam rose from the sink in the café's kitchen, but instead of warming the cold air in the room, it only made it damp and more miserable. The drinking glasses from last night felt like they had dew on them as Jenny picked them up to put them in the hot dishwater.

"I should have done these before I left last night," Jenny half apologized to Linda, who was operating the café with her boyfriend, Duane.

"Are you kidding? It would have been freezing in here then," Linda said as she reached up to the top shelf and brought down a couple of coffee cups. Linda wore thick, black leggings under a short black leather skirt. "It's not all that warm right now— would be colder if Duane hadn't made a large order of biscuits already this morning for the sheriff. The oven doesn't work right, but it does manage to heat the place some. Any of you want coffee?''

Linda spoke casually and seemingly to the air, but Jenny could see the young woman was not that unfocused. She kept looking at Laurel, Robert's friend.

Well, it wasn't so much that Linda was looking at Laurel as it was that she was studying the other woman. Linda, herself, had unnaturally red hair swept up in spikes that were tipped with gold glitter. Her lips were lined with black and one eyebrow was pierced so that a silver ring accented her pixie face.

She looked an unlikely woman to be so taken with Laurel, but she obviously was.

Jenny couldn't really blame her. Laurel looked as if she belonged in some classic movie. All she needed was a feather boa and one of those little dogs named Fluffy. Laurel should be lounging in a late-night dinner club. Actually, she would fit in almost anywhere better than this tiny café kitchen in Dry Creek, Montana, with its worn linoleum and chipped appliances.

Laurel wore a champagne silk dress. She had gold chains draped around her neck and diamond earrings dripping from her earlobes. Her lips weren't just red, they were glossy. She looked like she'd bitten into a large berry and kept the stain on her lips and fingertips. Her cheeks were smoothly colored and her platinum blond hair was ruffled expertly. There had to be mousse involved, but it didn't show. Laurel had the kind of casual elegance that costs a fortune.

If the woman didn't look so stiff, Jenny would have cheerfully hated her.

Jenny had deliberately decided not to compete with Laurel's style. Jenny was wearing a pair of black sweatpants, a white T-shirt and a large beige sweater. Nothing draped from her neck or dripped from her ears. Her only ornament was the small pin on her sweater announcing she had donated money to a Seattle animal shelter. Her only makeup was lip balm that she'd put on to keep her lips from becoming cracked in the winter weather. Her hair was clean and combed. That was about it.

"Or I could make you some tea if you'd like," Linda offered shyly, now addressing her remarks to the glamorous Laurel. "Something with an herbal spice to it maybe?"

"No, thanks, I couldn't possibly drink anything," Laurel said as she walked over to the window in the kitchen. "Unless you have some bottled water." She shuddered delicately. "I never drink tap water when I travel. It's one of those rules."

"That's for Mexico," Robert said as he walked into the kitchen. He was carrying a tub of plates that had been left out in the main part of the café after dinner last night. "This is Montana. They both start with *M*'s, but there's a big difference. Besides, you can drink boiled water anywhere. That kills the germs.''

Laurel shuddered again. ''But then they'd be dead in the water floating around. I couldn't possibly drink something with anything dead in it.''

Robert snorted. ''If you're that fussy, you'll have to stop breathing. There's germs everywhere—dead and alive.''

Laurel looked alarmed.

''Well, except for the really cold places like just outside the door,'' Robert continued. His mission for the morning was to get Jenny alone. So far, Jenny wouldn't even talk to him. He was hoping she would if they were alone. ''Real good clear air there.''

''But it's cold outside,'' Laurel wailed.

''That's what kills the germs,'' Robert responded matter-of-factly as he unloaded the plates from last night onto the counter. ''Talking about germs— these old plates are a hotbed of activity.''

Laurel moved back from the plastic tubs Robert was using to carry the dishes around. There was a tub for silverware, another for coffee mugs and another for punch cups. Half of the cups had lipstick stains on them and the other had spots of something or another.

''It's perfectly safe in here,'' Jenny said. The sudsy water felt good on her hands, but she was still glad for the long johns she had on under her sweatpants. "Restaurants have health inspectors that come around and check out things like that."

"They do?" Linda said with a gulp. The younger woman paused in the act of pulling a platter down from the cupboard. The eyebrow with the silver ring in it rose in panic.

"You mean you haven't?"

Linda shook her head. "Jazz—that's Duane—never said anything about health inspectors. Maybe he's done something about them. He takes care of all the business details. I'd better go ask him."

Jenny could hear Duane in the dining area of the restaurant putting salt and pepper shakers on the tables and getting the place ready to open. Linda walked out there and the mumbled sound of their voices reached back into the kitchen.

"I hope they don't get a fine or anything," Jenny worried aloud. She was automatically washing glasses as she worked. She set the glasses in a large tub so that they could be rinsed with scalding water before they were set to dry. She couldn't recall ever being in a restaurant that didn't have a machine that washed dishes. "I wonder if you need things like a sterilizing dishwasher machine to pass all the rules."

"I doubt they can afford to buy any equipment yet," Robert added. He doubted they had insurance, either. He'd have to remember to ask if they needed a small business loan. They'd never have collateral on their own to get one, but from what he'd seen they had a good shot at making a sound business.

"I'm surprised no health inspector has shown up already. They can just come unannounced. Maybe they do it different when you're not in a city." Jenny moved one of the tubs so she could start on the silverware.

"Maybe." Robert shrugged as he wrapped one dish towel around his hand and offered another towel to Laurel.

"For me?" Laurel's voice came out in a surprised squeak. She backed farther away from Robert. "But I can't—I've never even—not even at home. Why, I have a housekeeper."

By the time Laurel finished talking, she was at the doorway between the café's kitchen and its main dining room.

"I need to go to the house for something." Laurel managed to smile as she stepped into the other room.

"I thought that'd scare her off," Robert said as he picked up a bowl from the rack of dishes to be dried. He rubbed the towel around its edges. "She's not used to doing dishes."

"And you are?" Jenny looked at him skeptically. She still couldn't believe how competently and willingly he was working. She couldn't have paid anyone to work harder than this rich man was doing.

Robert was standing in front of the counter where the dried dishes were setting. He had modified his tuxedo when he came over to the café. He'd taken off the black jacket and was wearing a yellow sweatshirt that had been hanging on a nail by the kitchen door. It had paint splatters on it. Jazz had said he'd used it when he painted the café and had not gotten around to throwing it away yet. Jenny noted that the shirt had a tear under the armhole and a burn spot where Jazz had leaned too close to the stove.

Robert no longer looked like a rich man. His hair was mussed where he'd wrapped one of Mrs. Hargrove's wool scarves around his head because he was walking between the barn and the café bringing over the dirty dishes. The weather outside was frigid. The cold air made his cheeks blotchy.

It was more than that, however, Jenny thought. It was the look on his face that had changed. He no longer looked like a rich man because he no longer looked stressed. He smiled like he didn't have a dime in the world.

"Me? As a matter of fact, I've done a few dishes in my time," Robert answered, and then plunged into his story. "Not so long ago, in fact, when I was visiting a friend of mine outside of Tucson."

"I can't believe any of your friends would ask you to help with the dishes."

"The dishes were the fun part. The warm water felt good on the calluses I got on my hands from chopping wood. Took me a while to get the hang of it all. Long steady strokes worked best. You build up a rhythm that way."

Jenny stopped washing dishes and turned her full attention to Robert.

There was only one explanation that came to mind. "You can't possibly have lost all your money!" He must gamble or something. "Is that why you need to be on that list at my sister's paper?"

"Lost it? I didn't lose any money. Fact is, the Buckwalter Foundation has made money this past year. How I don't know, at the rate we're giving it away. But, no, I didn't lose my money. And—let me say this again—I don't want to be on any list. I'm doing my best to get off of it."

Jenny heard the words, but she couldn't make sense of what he was saying.

"Well, if you're trying to get off that list, why did you kiss me?" Jenny held up a frying pan that she was cleaning and frowned at it fiercely. It was a solid cast-iron pan usually used for frying bacon. "You must have known I'd tell my sister."

Jenny brought the pan down to the counter and attacked it again with a wet dishrag. Cast iron couldn't be washed with the rest of the dishes. "Kissing me like that—how was that supposed to get you off the list? I thought you did it because you wanted to get *on* that list."

Robert watched Jenny scowl at the bottom of the

cast-iron pan. Her jaw was set, but a thin sheen of pink spread over her cheeks. She was flustered.

"You liked the kiss," Robert said.

Jenny looked up from her scouring and frowned at him. "I never said that."

"I'm going on faith." Robert felt like whistling. "If you hadn't liked it, you would have told your sister it was awful and you wouldn't even think that would help me get on that list."

Jenny kept the frown and added a full-blown blush. "I don't think—"

Robert put his fingers on her lips. "You don't need to think when it comes to kisses. Not then. Not now."

Robert bent his head and kissed Jenny. This time there were no cameras. No flashes. No audience. Just the two of them. And more steam than either one of them had ever seen before.

"The hot water's still running," Robert finally said as he pulled away. The frying pan was pressing against the hot water handle and a steady stream of scalding hot water was filling the air with clouds of moist steam. The steam made Jenny's cheeks pinker and her lips soft. "But hot water is good."

Robert bent to kiss Jenny again.

Jenny wondered what was wrong with her. Every time this man kissed her she got warmer and warmer. Last time it was the lights that had confused her and made her think she was near a crackling fire. This time it was the heat. How did it get so hot in this kitchen when it was ten below zero outside?

"Tropical," Jenny whispered. She was trying to grab hold of her sanity and keep it. She felt as if she were under a spell that stopped time and created puffs of white steam. "It's tropical in here."

"Perfect. It's perfect in here," Robert said as he pulled away.

The moisture in the air made Jenny's hair curve toward her face. Robert knew that somewhere in the chef apron pocket lurked a hair net that would squash her hair even further. Jenny wore no makeup. The pink in her cheeks was from the heat and not from any brush.

"You're perfect."

Jenny started. The spell was broken. "No one's perfect."

No one except Laurel, Jenny thought to herself. She could hardly believe Robert Buckwalter III was happy to help with the dishes. But there was no way she'd ever believe he would prefer the hired help to someone like Laurel. Laurel might be overdressed and she might be a snob, but she still was his kind. They belonged to the same social set. It was clear.

"Why are you helping with the dishes?"

Robert looked up.

"It doesn't seem fair," she said. "Your mother is paying me to do the dishes and then you're helping me anyway."

Robert shrugged. "I want to."

Jenny didn't have an answer to that one. But she knew for sure something was off center. Who wanted to do dishes?

There were twenty bins of dirty dishes. Jenny thought Robert would lose interest before the second bin was emptied. The novelty of doing dishes wore off fast, even to people who hadn't done many in their life.

But Robert stayed. He washed dishes and talked about his months in the desert. He explained about Bob and how good it felt to be free of the life of a rich man. Then he talked about his childhood and how much he still missed his father. He was curious about her brothers and sisters. She told him. He wanted to know how she felt about her parents. She told him.

All the while, he washed and dried dishes. The stack of damp dish towels grew, but he didn't complain.

The phone call came when they were almost done with the dishes. It was ten-thirty and Linda and Jazz had started their famous spaghetti sauce simmering.

"Oh, hi." The phone was on the counter closest to Jenny and she clicked on it first. It was her sister.

Jenny was still standing in front of the sink, but she moved back a little and used one hand to untie the apron strings wrapped around her waist.

"I'm calling to talk to Robert Buckwalter. Is he around?" her sister asked.

"Yes." Jenny smiled over at Robert. "He's right here."

"With you?" Jenny's sister dropped to a cautious whisper. "Are you saying he's with you?"

"Mmm-hmm."

"You two aren't dancing or kissing or anything? I always seem to have this bad timing and catch you just when things are getting good."

"We're washing dishes."

"Dishes! You've got to be kidding. I thought you'd at least be sitting down and talking or something."

"We have been talking. Just standing up and doing the dishes at the same time."

Robert almost winced. He hadn't realized until just now how far from the mark his romancing was when viewed objectively. Women were independent these days, but they liked to know a man wasn't totally without manners. He looked around. He didn't even have a chair to offer her.

He'd already called his pilot friend and made an arrangement to have him fly over and make a supply drop near Robert's plane early tomorrow morning. Robert had even made plans to have his plane moved so it would be out in the open and make a good drop site.

But Robert suddenly realized he had a lot riding

on that plane drop. The more he talked with Jenny, the more he cared what she thought of him. A few boxes of food—most of it for other people, and hungry teenagers at that—might not be enough of a gift to say he cared about her.

"Hey." Robert walked over and tapped Jazz on the shoulder. The younger man was standing at a side counter, chopping onions to the beat of the music coming out of the headphones he wore.

"Yeah." The younger man pushed an earphone away from his ear so he could hear. He put a hand up and brushed away some tears from his eyes. "Man, them onions'll get you. Ever chop an onion?"

"Not that I remember."

"Oh, you'd remember all right."

Robert didn't have time to talk about onions. Jenny would only talk to her sister for so long before the sister would want to talk business with him. "You don't happen to have carnations, do you?"

The younger man looked up. "Do they make the tears stop? I've heard there's ways to chop onions without the tears. Never heard of carnations. Do you eat them, or what?"

"I don't know anything about onions and you shouldn't eat carnations for any reason. I'm just asking about carnations. A lot of restaurants put cut flowers on the table. I thought you might have carnations you use."

''We have red candles.''

Robert had never heard of a bouquet of red candles, but he was pretty sure it wouldn't work.

''People like them,'' the younger man said. ''They're kind of romantic.''

''I don't suppose you have any vine-ripened tomatoes, do you?''

Jazz shook his head. ''We've got them in cans. Sauce or paste.''

A can of tomato sauce wouldn't make it, either.

''What do you give your girlfriend when you want to get her something nice?''

''I've had Earl put aside a set of tires.''

Robert wondered if he was talking to the right guy. ''Tires?''

Jazz ducked and then offered hesitantly, ''They're snow tires. You need them around here this time of year and hers are thin. Besides, I was also going to give her a nose ring, too. She's been wanting one.''

The door to the café opened and the FBI agent and Francis Elkton, the rancher's sister, came inside. They were talking quietly to each other and Robert noticed they had snowflakes on their hair.

''Gotta go,'' Jazz said as he went back into the front part of the café. ''Customers, you know.''

Robert nodded. He wondered if that FBI agent had any ideas about how to get a romantic gift in the middle of Montana with no stores in sight. There weren't even wildflowers to gather. It was just snow and rocks outside.

Linda picked up a pot of coffee and followed Jazz out of the kitchen.

At least, Robert thought, he was now alone with Jenny. That was something. He could see the happiness in her face while she talked with her sister. He'd seen the affection on her face earlier when she spoke of her sisters and brothers.

Now Jenny was someone who knew what it meant to love other people. He wondered if she had gotten any of that knowledge from reading the Bible like he'd done last night. He wouldn't be surprised if she had.

"My sister needs to know what story you're offering," Jenny called over to Robert. "She said the senior editors have been asking her."

Jenny could hardly believe that Robert didn't want to be on that list. But her sister was adamant. She wasn't sure she could help him get off, but she was going to try.

Jenny gave the phone to Robert.

"Have they said they'd trade stories?" Robert asked in the phone.

"They said it needs to be something big—bigger than the bachelor story."

"I could tell them what I've been up to for the past five months—about being in the desert."

"Let me see." The sister covered the mouthpiece

on the phone and was obviously talking to someone. Finally she came back. "They said not unless it involves you eating wild locusts and taking religious vows to be a monk—a bed of nails would help."

Robert snorted. "Help who?"

He thought further. "I did have a persecutor in the desert. A farmyard rooster. A cranky bird. Bit me once."

Robert heard the muffled sounds of talking at the other end again. "They asked if the bird has been certified by a priest as being possessed or if it's been abducted by space aliens."

"What would space aliens want with Charlie?"

"Maybe they'd want to study him."

"He's just a farm rooster." Robert was defeated. He was half tempted to say that he was in the midst of a religious makeover, but he didn't want to joke around with that. The tabloids never knew when to stop. They knew what they wanted and it had to be sensational. "I could c﹍er a Buckwalter Grant to space aliens. Broadcast it on radio frequencies. Ask them to come pick up a million-dollar check. Get some of those groups involved who scan the airwaves for messages."

"Hmmm, not bad." He heard more muffled sounds as the sister conferred with her editors. "Not believable enough."

"Not believable! You've got to be kidding!"

"Well, we need our readers to trust us," the sister

said a little louder than normal. "We don't fool around about money." Her voice dipped and she whispered. "I think they're holding out for the story of your engagement to Laurel what's-her-name. That's what they really want."

"I'm not engaged."

"Their sources tell them otherwise."

"Laurel is their source."

"I can't confirm that."

"You don't need to. I know what's going on."

"Do you?"

Robert wasn't sure when they'd stopped talking about the story and had started talking about him. The sister didn't even try to hide her resentment.

"I can't control what Laurel is saying." Robert knew he was talking to both sisters. "I never proposed to Laurel. Cross my heart and hope to die—on a bed of nails if necessary. I'm telling the truth. I haven't even seen Laurel for months. I think we went out on two dates in high school. That's it. I'm not even her type and she's certainly not mine. She's a publicity hound. She'll drop the idea of marrying me quick enough once I'm off that cursed list."

"Hmmm."

Robert thought the sister was softening.

"Still, you could use the story," the sister offered kindly. "Even a solid lead of an engagement—like 'sources close to'—that kind of a thing. And a couple of photos of you kissing. Really, even the photos themselves would do. It would be enough to keep the editors happy.''

"How much time do I have to come up with something else?''

"We can give you until tomorrow at noon. If we absolutely need to we could go another day, but that's pushing back our press time.''

"I'll call before then.''

Robert handed the phone back to Jenny. He knew he couldn't use a fake engagement story. It would ruin any chance he had with Jenny. But he had a day to think of something else.

Robert wondered if space aliens could be bribed to come down and take Charlie for a spin on a UFO. It wouldn't even need to be a big UFO as long as Robert could get a picture of it.

Chapter Nine

"Flint Harris, FBI." The man seemed to walk into the kitchen and flip his badge open in one seamless movement. He stopped in front of Robert.

"Mind telling me what your business is in Dry Creek?" The agent looked like he'd had a tough night, but his voice was one hundred percent official.

"Me?" Robert was surprised. He had walked over to the tall cupboard to put back some bowls.

"It's my fault." Duane the Jazz Man followed the agent inside. "The man asked me if anyone had been asking funny questions and I told him you had been."

"Me?"

"Yeah, the carnations that you're not supposed to eat and the cans of tomatoes—the sauce kind and the paste."

Robert winced. He set the bowls down on the counter. "I was trying to think of a gift for someone special."

The FBI agent looked at him even more suspiciously. "Someone special? Cans of tomatoes? Carnations? Aren't you the rich guy?"

Robert nodded. "Sometimes a gift should count for more than its price tag."

The agent snorted and looked over at Jenny.

He lowered his voice so only the men could hear. "I thought a guy like you'd go more for orchids or roses or something fancy that men like me haven't even heard of—night crawlers or something."

"Night crawlers are worms."

"I mean night bloomers." The agent shook his head. "See what Francis does to me? I can't even think straight. But I can't make any headway with her. You'd think we'd never been, well, you know. Turns out we were actually married—but you'd never know it now. I was hoping someone would have flowers."

"You see any floral shops around?"

"I know." The agent looked at the woman who'd come to the kitchen door. It was Francis. His face softened to mush. "I was just hoping. Sometimes a guy could use a little help, if you know what I mean."

Robert knew exactly what he meant. He nodded toward Duane. "He's reduced to snow tires."

Duane ducked his head in acknowledgment. "And a nose ring."

"Well, I guess I should keep my mind on business anyway," the agent said. "Unless I miss my guess, this rustling thing is going to break wide open here soon, and when it does the citizens of Dry Creek are going to find some nasty surprises."

Robert lifted his eyebrow.

"I figure there has to be someone local involved. And from the amount of information that has been sent along about Dry Creek, it's either someone who knows everything really well or it's more than one person. Maybe a group of people."

"Here?"

The agent nodded.

"But all of the men I've seen are ranchers themselves. They know what the rustling means to others. And the women, well—" Robert tried to picture Mrs. Hargrove leading a band of female informants. They could knit in code and send neck scarves out with the information. "I don't think so."

"Still, keep your ears open. And let me know if you hear of anyone asking unusual questions." The agent looked over at Duane. "Unusual questions about cattle—who's got winter pasture where and who's moving their herds at what time. Those kinds of questions. Even weather questions might lead to something. A lot of the cattle movements are determined by weather."

Duane nodded. "Old man Gossett would be the one asking about the weather. But that's just because his television is broken. He comes over and asks almost every day. Then he moans about it. Snow. Rain. It doesn't matter. He complains. The amount of time he spends worrying—I guess it's just his way."

That was the old man he'd invited to dinner last night. Robert remembered him clearly. "I expect the cold weather troubles his joints."

The FBI agent grunted. "He might be someone to watch at that if he's talking to lots of people."

"Oh, he don't so much talk as listen," Duane corrected. "Sort of listens on the side if you know what I mean."

"Eavesdropping?"

Duane nodded. "Everybody knows. They don't pay him much attention anymore. They just let him be. Who's he gonna tell anyway? Never talks to nobody."

"That kind of listening is the most dangerous. People don't watch their tongues around him. Besides, he's getting money from someplace. I figured he was living on Social Security until last night. Did you see him in his new coat? He wouldn't get money to buy stuff like that on his government check."

"I gave him the coat." Robert doubted the older

man had the connections to be a rustler. He seemed more like a lonely old man than a criminal.

"Nice coat. Expensive."

Robert hoped that meant the old man got off the suspects list, but he couldn't read the agent's face. "It'll keep him warm."

The agent nodded and looked more closely at Robert. "What are you doing here in that getup?" He jerked his head toward the sweatshirt.

Robert knew the sweatshirt was paint spotted and yellow. Bright yellow. But it was warm and that was enough. "I'm here doing dishes. A tuxedo seemed a little overdressed."

The agent looked over at Jenny and then back at Robert.

The agent lowered his voice. "I see. Not a bad idea. You might not need roses at that. Never knew a woman that could be mad at a man when he was doing dishes for her. Good move."

Robert looked at Jenny. She was fifteen feet away from him and she might as well be fifteen miles. She'd stopped talking to her sister and was back to scowling at that frying pan.

"I could still use some roses," Robert said. "I don't think there's enough dirty dishes in the world to win her over."

"I'll let you know if I find a magician who can pull a few roses out of his hat."

"Same here." Robert didn't tell the agent that the

last time he had given roses to a woman she'd been insulted. She had thought roses were too common a flower to come from a Buckwalter. "Any particular color you'd like?"

"Yellow. Francis loves yellow roses—or at least she did when I knew her back in high school."

Robert made a mental note to call that pilot he'd hired and see if he could put three dozen long-stem roses in the drop he was planning for tomorrow morning. A dozen deep red ones for Jenny. A dozen yellow for the agent to give to his Francis. And— he looked over at Linda and Duane assessingly— maybe a lavender bouquet for the young couple.

"What was that about?" Jenny asked when Robert came back to the sink. Without waiting for him to answer, she continued as though she'd rehearsed the words. "You can do it, you know. If you want to run that engagement story, that's fine."

Robert couldn't see Jenny's face. She was looking down at something in the sink.

"Not that it's any of my business," she added with a quick look up at his face before she looked down again. "I just want you to know that no one who knows you would blame you. And you could always tell them the truth later. People would understand. I know you want off the list."

Robert laid down the dish towel he'd been holding. The dishwater no longer steamed up from the sink. The pink in Jenny's cheeks was natural. Lashes half hid her brown eyes. Her lips curved in a hint of a smile. Robert thought she looked absolutely adorable.

"I'll find another way to get off the list."

"My sister says there is no other way."

"We'll see." Robert comforted himself and her. Then he added impulsively, "I'm going to pray about it."

Jenny looked up in surprise. "I didn't know people like you prayed about anything."

"I've become a new man. That's what I've been telling you all morning."

"And the 'new you' prays?"

Robert nodded. "The new me has to pray. Sometimes I don't have a clue. Not that I always knew everything before—but, now, well what kind of a fool wouldn't pray? It's like having a million dollars in the bank and never writing a check."

"You've always been rich."

Robert nodded. "Money, yes. But prayers, no. I'm beginning to think that—in the important things—I've lived like some fool who's starving to death in a fully stocked deli just because he doesn't know how to stand in line."

Jenny decided Robert no longer had the heart of a rich man. He'd become a regular kind of guy. He'd even admitted he might need help with his life. She liked this new guy much better than the rich guy he used to be.

She hoped she didn't like him too much. Just because Robert Buckwalter changed one day didn't mean he couldn't change right back the next.

The day divided itself into meals. Jenny couldn't think beyond that. The teenagers at the ranch were all coming into Dry Creek for lunch and to clean up the decorations from last night's dance.

"We have four hamburger patties left and seven hot dogs," Linda said. The younger woman was looking in the top compartment of the old refrigerator. "We aren't able to keep too much on hand in the way of supplies in this old thing. We're having trouble with the stove, too. Plus we're out of almost everything. The spaghetti sauce we have going is straight marinara—not even mushrooms. There's no potatoes for French fries or ice cream for shakes."

"That's all it seems the kids want to eat," Jenny worried aloud. She'd finished wiping down the counter and was folding the dishrag. "I know they'll eat anything if they're hungry enough, but I hate to put them back on the macaroni-and-cheese diet they've had for the past week."

"Ah—Sylvia called from the ranch," Linda said hesitantly as she stood up and closed the refrigerator door. "That's why we started the spaghetti sauce. She said they used the last of the boxes of macaroni and cheese yesterday. A quick lunch for the boys. There's none left. And the spaghetti sauce won't be enough for everyone."

"We're doomed then."

Jenny walked over to a kitchen chair and sat down.

"I learned how to make Navajo fry bread when I was in the desert," Robert offered. He finished drying the last cup. "I've checked and we have what we need. We could make it a cultural ethnic kind of a night."

"Spaghetti's Italian—we could put an extra dose of the authentic seasoning," Linda offered. She walked to the stove and opened the lid on a pot. "No one will have a full serving, but we could stretch it so they each have a small plate of it. We have a big jar of kosher pickles, too—they'd fit for the Jewish touch."

"I could make a Mexican flan for dessert—we've got lots of eggs and milk still," Jenny added. She went to a cupboard and looked inside. The cupboard was empty except for dishes. "It's not much, but—"

"Kids love an adventure," Robert folded his dish towel. "We'll sell them on the fun of it."

"Duane can play his guitar. He knows all kinds of music. Some sounds like mariachi music from Mexico. He might be able to do some Navajo drumming for the fry bread, too."

"It just might work." Jenny closed the cupboard.

"If anyone has a sturdy box, we can make a homemade piñata. Fill it with whatever's handy."

Robert walked to the pantry. "I bet there's something in here to use."

"We've got those old candy canes left over from Christmas. I think they're in there." Linda opened a side cupboard near the refrigerator. "Ah, here they are. We had Santa giving them out."

Linda pulled out a large plastic bag filled with candy canes. "Maybe we shouldn't give them to the kids—" she looked up at Jenny "—you know our Santa was a hit man, don't you? Went right after the Christmas angel with a gun! If it wasn't for the preacher, she'd be dead. 'Course now she's married to the preacher." Linda paused to look into the other room at Duane. "It was so romantic. Him risking his life for her."

"But he could have been killed," Jenny protested. She didn't want the younger woman to be under the wrong impression. There was nothing romantic about life-and-death danger. "I heard the preacher didn't even have a gun."

Robert envied the man who had almost died. Now there was a man who had a chance to impress the woman he chose. No wonder he had been able to close the deal with a wedding band. Somehow, carving up carrots and washing dishes seemed too tame by comparison.

"I told Mrs. Hargrove I'd check with her about now," Jenny said as she walked over to the café's back door, the one that led off of the kitchen. "She's promised to give the church a quick cleaning for services tomorrow and I wanted to be sure she got over there all right.''

Jenny pulled a parka off a peg by the door and slid her arms into the sleeves.

"I can get her there," Robert offered. "You can stay here. It's slippery cold out there and you don't even have snow boots."

"Neither do you." Jenny pulled a wool scarf from the large pocket of the coat and wrapped the scarf around her head.

"But I've got bigger feet." Robert pulled a man's jacket off of the peg. The jacket was denim lined with some kind of furry material. "I can keep my balance better in the icy places."

"Nonsense."

Two minutes later, Jenny was lying on the icy ground on her back, looking up at the sky. She'd gone outside anyway, not even waiting for Robert. She didn't want him to think she was incapable of walking a few steps in the snow.

Well, so much for that, she thought as she winced. After the fall she'd taken, he'd think that incompetence was the least of her worries.

"I knew you should have waited," Robert said as he stepped out of the kitchen door and knelt down beside her. "Where does it hurt?"

"My left ankle."

"Here, let me see." Robert slipped off his gloves and rolled down her thick socks.

For a second, her leg tingled from the cold air and then Robert wrapped his warm hands around it and gently probed. "No broken bones."

"I'll be all right." Jenny could almost be back in the kitchen with the steam. She was starting to feel warm again. "Just help me up. I'll be fine."

"You'll be no such thing," Robert said as he rolled her sock back up to cover her leg. "You've got a sprain. You'll need to stay off your foot for a while."

Jenny looked around her. She was sprawled in front of the café.

The main street of Dry Creek wasn't so much a street as it was the widening of the road that cut through town. The barn and the church were on one side with a few houses between them and the café was on the other side with a few more houses.

Jenny was ten feet from the café, which would place her on the shoulder of the road, she supposed. It was hard to tell where the road began and ended because of the ruts in the snow left from all the cars and trucks that had been parked here last night. The ruts were now covered with fresh snow so the whole area looked soft, white and lumpy.

"It's not so bad." Jenny looked up at Robert. The midmorning sun gave off a subdued white light but it still reflected off the sprinkling of blond hairs on his head. She'd never seen him in the full sun before. That must be why she'd never noticed before that there was any blond in the dark of his hair. She wondered how it had gotten so blond in places. "It must be the desert sun."

Robert's eyes were bluer than the sky. Jenny decided she'd have to remember to tell her sister about them. "Does the desert change the color of blue?"

The blue in Robert's eyes turned gray and his hands left her ankle.

"Did you hit your head?" Robert's hands cupped Jenny's skull gently and started to feel their way around her forehead. "Can you count to ten?"

"Of course."

"Backward?"

"I didn't hit my head." Jenny's hair was on fire. She couldn't breathe. She was undone. Something in the universe was very unfair. She was no match for Robert Buckwalter. She'd done fine with him until she'd really looked at him. Now she needed mercy. She needed air. Her sister was right. The man was an Adonis.

"Count to ten then."

"Huh?"

"Ten. Nine—"

"You need to leave me." Jenny finally gasped the words out. She needed to get a handle on herself. Even if she hadn't hit her head, maybe she was sick or something. "I can't breathe."

"It's your ribs!"

Robert didn't leave. Nor did he take his hands away. He only moved them to gently feel along her rib cage. "They seem fine."

"They *are* fine. It's you." Jenny's cheeks flamed. She hadn't felt this awkward since she was thirteen. "You need to leave so I can breathe."

"Oh."

Robert rocked back on his heels. He took his hands off her ribs.

Jenny closed her eyes and concentrated on taking slow, deep breaths. She was just rattled, that's all. Her sister was right. She, Jenny, needed to get out more. If just looking at an attractive man sent her into a tailspin, it was only proof that she needed to date more. She'd do that, just as soon as she got back to the safety of Seattle.

"Better?"

Jenny opened her eyes and nodded.

"You're sure you don't hurt anywhere but the ankle?"

"I'm sure. I just got the wind knocked out of me."

Jenny forced a smile on her face. That was it. It was the shock of falling down that suddenly made the man look so gorgeous. Maybe it was like one of those near-death experiences. Not as serious, of course. But something that happened that made the next few minutes of life look more attractive than it really was. If she'd been looking at a cactus, she'd have thought it was diamond studded. It was just a case of misperception.

"I'll be fine. Just give me a hand up."

Robert grunted. "Even if everything else is fine, you still can't walk on that ankle for a while."

"Well, I can't just sit here in the snow," Jenny said as she sat up and lifted her arm for assistance. "Besides, I have lunch to worry about."

Robert took her arm and helped her stand.

Jenny had snow stuck to the back of her coat and the back of her sweatpants, but she didn't bend to brush it off.

"You don't need to worry about lunch. Or dinner," Robert said as he slipped his arm under one of hers and scooped her up into his arms.

"Oh." Jenny blinked.

Jenny blinked again. The sun was still behind the man. That must be why she suddenly felt so giddy.

Chapter Ten

"Another cup of cocoa?"

Jenny looked up at Robert. She was lying on the couch in Mrs. Hargrove's living room. The same couch that Robert had laid her down on over eight hours ago when she'd twisted her ankle. He'd only let her get up a few times to hobble around the house briefly. He'd spent all of that time, except for when she took a nap, being her nurse.

"I can't drink another drop." Jenny liked this Robert better—the one inside the house. The sun didn't play with his hair and confuse her. He looked more like a normal man in the shadows of the house. "You don't need to bother, you know."

"I know," Robert said the rest of the words along with her "—you're fine."

"Well, I am. The swelling has already gone

down. And everyone says it's only a sprain. I could be walking on it by now.''

Jenny looked at the empty cup she'd just set on the coffee table. Robert had originally pulled the coffee table close, saying she needed a place to set her cup.

That was six cups ago.

The table had served as his command center. First, he'd brought ice for her foot. And a pillow. Then a cup of tea with honey in it. Then he'd gotten a thick salve from the hardware store and rubbed it on her ankle. He wouldn't let her look at the label, but Jenny strongly suspected the salve was something ordinarily used on cattle. Before she could ask, he was off to bring back a cup of cocoa and some toast.

''I wanted marshmallows, but there weren't any,'' Robert apologized. He had a towel draped over his arm like a high-class waiter. ''The closest I could get was buying a breath mint from one of the kids. Stirred it around and it made a mint-chocolate cocoa.''

Jenny took a sip. The liquid was rich and warm. And just a little minty. ''It's perfect.''

''I'm still learning.'' Robert sat down on a straight-back chair that he'd pulled near the couch earlier so they could play a game of cards. ''Mrs. Hargrove has been teaching me all about preparing food. She's on the care of pots and pans now. Never realized there was so much to this cooking business."

"I never realized Mrs. Hargrove cared so much about her pots and pans."

Robert grinned. "Not sure she does. She's using them to teach me lessons, I think."

"About?"

"Gratitude, for starters. Have you ever thought about where we'd be without a pot or a pan to our name?"

Jenny shrugged. "We'd have to cook stuff on a stick, I guess."

"We wouldn't have soups or stews." Robert began reciting the list. "No gravies. No puddings." He paused. "Tell that to your sister. Maybe next time she should impersonate a cookware salesman. It's more basic."

"She shouldn't impersonate anyone. And I've talked to her about it."

Robert grinned.

Jenny eyed him suspiciously. "What's that for?"

"I'm just practicing doing what Mrs. Hargrove recommends."

"And?"

Robert paused, then grinned wider. "I'm thinking how grateful I am for the fact that you always speak your mind."

"My sister wasn't. She thought I was bossy."

"Well, tell your sister I'd trade places with her

any day in that regard. When you're rich, you never know if people mean what they say or not. No one dares to be bossy and I've kind of missed it.''

Jenny looked at Robert more closely. He just wasn't what she expected when she thought of a rich man. He wasn't living up to her stereotypes at all. "Have you ever abandoned a kitten?"

"Me? Never."

"A dog?"

"Of course not."

"Any other pet that you may have owned?"

"The closest thing I've had to a pet is a rooster named Charlie. And he wasn't mine. He just lived next door."

"Well, were you good to him?"

Robert chuckled. "He was the sorriest excuse for a neighbor I've ever seen. He was loud. Demanding. Inconsiderate. Worse than a boom box playing at dawn. But I still gave him his handful of grain every single day that I was there. Even the day he pecked at me.''

"Good." Jenny lay back on the pillows on the couch.

"Good he almost bit me?"

"No, good because you fed him and didn't hold a grudge. He was only being what he was—a chicken. It's his destiny.''

"He could have been a chicken without pecking at me. He's a chicken—I don't think he has a destiny. But, even if he did, just following your destiny isn't enough. Sometimes it's nothing but an excuse not to do better. That's why I want you to know I'm working on changing myself, Jenny. I know I haven't always been the most thoughtful, considerate guy in the universe, but I believe that—with God's help—I can change.''

"Mrs. Hargrove tells me you're a fine young man." Jenny bent down to drink out of her cocoa cup. That's not all Mrs. Hargrove had said. She'd also told Jenny that Robert was a man in a million and she should snap him up before someone like that Laurel made good on her threat and got her hands on him. Jenny wondered how Mrs. Hargrove thought she, Jenny, was supposed to do that. She might as well have commanded her to sing an opera or float in the air.

"Mrs. Hargrove is prejudiced," Robert said.

Jenny raised an eyebrow.

"While you took your nap earlier, I went over and cleaned the church for her. I even followed her instructions.''

Jenny raised her eyebrow even more.

"That's right. There are lessons to be learned in cleaning, too. Mostly they've got to do with being humble and using the right bottle of stuff when you scrub the floor on your hands and knees.''

"Mrs. Hargrove shouldn't be scrubbing those floors on her knees. Not at her age.''

"I know. I've already called in an order for a small commercial floor scrubber. It'll work to her specifications. She doesn't believe in hand mops. She thinks they miss the little spots."

"What are the lessons there?"

"Thinking some sins are so small they don't need God's forgiveness." Robert smiled. "I know it's a little corny, but I like what she's done with her life. She's made everything have meaning. So cleaning a dirty floor in the church isn't just about scrubbing. It's about honoring God. It's about paying attention to the small stuff. No wonder she goes about her days like a drill sergeant. Everything is important."

The day had long since drifted into early evening and the light in the living room had become even dimmer. Shadows filled the corners. The couch where Jenny lay was square in front of the fireplace that took up one wall of the room. A row of windows took up another wall and a dozen framed snapshots took up the final wall.

"I wonder what my life will be like when I'm as old as Mrs. Hargrove and I look back over it." Robert stood up and switched on the floor lamp that stood at the end of the couch. "Wonder what my picture wall will look like."

"Lots of shots of you handing out money—lots of those big checks like they show on the lottery."

Jenny kept holding on to the differences between them. Robert had money with a capital *M*. She had loose change. She was walking through quicksand and she needed a firm place to stand. The difference in their bank accounts was as good a place as any.

"We all write checks and spend money." Robert sat down on the floor near the sofa where she was lying. "When it all ends, we've either spent or given away every dime we've ever made. If we haven't, the government does it for us. I might have more dimes to give away than most, but it all ends the same. It's all gone to one place or the other. We sure aren't taking it with us."

"Those kids that are over at Garth's don't believe that." Jenny wondered if Robert could really be so blind to the difference that money made in someone's life. "They're not worried about taking it with them, but they've seen what being poor can do to a person."

"And I've seen what being rich can do to a person."

"Most people would pick rich."

"I suppose so." Robert nodded and then looked around at the room. The light of evening was dimming even further. The light gave a soft circle of warmth. Mrs. Hargrove had gone to the café to help prepare the dinner for the teenagers tonight. She had convinced Laurel to go with her, telling her the ranch hands would be disappointed if she didn't come.

Robert was alone with Jenny and he was tired of talking about money.

"I'm going to make a fire in the fireplace. Maybe light a few candles," Robert said as he walked out into the kitchen. "I'll need to bring in some wood first."

Jenny nodded. She was grateful he was stepping outside. She pulled the cell phone off the coffee table and quickly dialed.

"Yeah, it's me." She spoke softly when her sister answered and then she listened a bit. "No, he's outside. That's why I called. Have you had a chance to talk to your source?"

"My source isn't the main source. I want you to know that. But the woman did know Robert some years ago. She gave a good recommendation. I don't think you need to worry. Your Robert sounds like a nice guy."

"He's not my Robert and I'm out of my league here."

"Well, short of hiring a private detective to dig through his trash, I think we'll just have to assume he's datable. That's what you really want to know, isn't it?"

"We can't date—I mean, look at the differences. Besides, Dad wouldn't approve."

"Dad's not lying there on a sofa with a drop-dead gorgeous Adonis cooking for him. Is he wearing a shirt?"

"Of course he's wearing a shirt! It's twenty degrees below outside."

"Oh," her sister said and then brightened. "But he is cooking for you. That's so romantic."

"He's only done tea, cocoa and dry toast. He worries about my foot. It's more medical than romantic."

"Forget the foot. You don't get cocoa in hospitals. Tea and dry toast maybe, but cocoa is definitely romantic. Did it have a marshmallow?"

"No, it had a breath mint."

"Now that's romantic. I'll bet he's kissed you again."

"No."

Her sister was silent before she said cautiously, "But you're lying on the sofa."

"With ice on my foot."

"You don't still have that hair net on, do you?"

"No. And Mrs. Hargrove even brought me a comb-and-brush set so my hair looks all right."

"Then why isn't he kissing you?"

"I asked him about money."

"Forget about his money. Pretend he's poor. Absolutely broke."

Jenny snorted. "You don't just pretend someone like that is poor. It's condescending. You talk about the problem like a mature adult."

"You're talking about problems?" Jenny's sister

wailed. "Don't talk about problems. This is a date. It isn't supposed to have problems."

"It's not a date. He's just being kind to me because I sprained my ankle."

"You. Him. Alone. Hot cocoa. I'm counting that as a date. I've already reported to Mom. She's been worried that you're not dating enough."

"I'm dating just fine."

"Well, now you are since you've met Robert Buckwalter the—"

"I know."

"—the Third. Say what do you call him anyway?"

"Bob. He wants to be called Bob."

"Really? He never mentioned that in any of his interviews."

"That's because he's a changed man now."

"Really? He never mentioned changed in his interviews."

Jenny could hear her sister flipping through papers.

"You're sure he said changed?" her sister asked.

"Yes."

"Well, I wonder what a man like that would want to change about himself? He's rich. He's gorgeous. He's kind."

"He wants to be Bob."

"And he hasn't kissed you again?"

Jenny shook her head. "No."

"Hmmm, I wonder why—"

"He's been reading the Bible—"

"He's not becoming a priest, is he? That would really upset the editors. We couldn't name a priest as the number one bachelor."

"I thought you were going to back off on that bachelor thing."

"My editors aren't sure. I've tried to back them off, but then I stopped. I think when I tried extra hard to convince them, they called their source and asked a few questions and now it's all gotten confused."

"What's confusing? The man has perfectly sound reasons for not wanting to be on that list. I'd think they'd respect his privacy and do what he wants."

"That's just it. They're not sure why he wants what he says he wants. They think he might be creating a—what did they call it?—a smoke screen. A diversion of sorts to cover up the real story."

"And what's the real story? They're not still on that engagement thing, are they? Bob, I mean Robert, he sure doesn't act engaged."

Her sister was silent for a minute. "They've had another tip. Something their source said by mistake."

"Robert thinks their source is Laurel. So if she claims they're engaged, I suppose they would listen."

"No, they've decided he's not engaged to Laurel.

She's worked for them for years and they know her pretty well.''

''Well, good—at least that's settled.''

''They still think he's engaged.''

Jenny's heart sank. She hadn't considered that. She'd been so worried he was involved with Laurel, she didn't count the billion other women in the world who would want to marry the man.

''Is she someone nice?'' Jenny asked stiffly.

The room had suddenly gotten colder. Jenny told herself she shouldn't begrudge the man a fiancée. She was, after all, the hired help. It was none of her business.

''I think she's nice.''

''Oh.'' Jenny blinked back a tear.

''They think it's you.''

Jenny heard her sister's voice at the same time as Robert came back into the living room with his arms full of logs for the fireplace.

''Me?'' Jenny squeaked, and blinked again.

Robert walked over to the fireplace and put the logs down. ''Let me say hi to your sister. I'm assuming that's her. She's the only one who calls on that number. I'm wondering what the editors have told her. Maybe I should talk to her.''

Jenny blinked again. ''She can't talk to you.''

''It's okay,'' her sister said on the other end of the phone. ''I won't tell him about the—you know what. Besides, I know it's not true. I just couldn't convince my editors. They think that because you're my sister, I'm protecting you from the media frenzy.''

Jenny looked up at Robert as he walked back to the sofa. The outside cold had added white to his forehead and pink to his cheeks. His chin was strong with a faint smudge of whiskers covering it. He'd left his head bare when he went outside and a few specks of snow glistened on his black hair. The lamp near the sofa gave a soft light that left the room full of partial shadows. Jenny wished she could go hide in one of them.

''Is your sister on a deadline?''

Jenny's mouth was dry. Robert's blue eyes had deepened to midnight and they were looking down at her. ''What?''

''Is that why she can't talk to me? I thought your sister might be writing something. Last time I talked to her she said they were giving her the simple assignments. Grunt work she called it. She's just waiting for her big break.'' Robert smiled at Jenny. ''I hope she gets it. She's a nice kid.''

''Yeah.'' Jenny swallowed.

''If it's the deadline, tell her I'll only take a minute. I know how it is when every minute counts.''

''It's not that. It's just that there's nothing new.'' Jenny forced her voice to be bright. ''The editors are still making a decision. I asked. There's nothing new at all.''

"Oh, well, thanks." Robert turned to walk back to the fireplace. "That's what I wanted to know."

Jenny looked down at the phone in her hand as though it had turned into something strange and exotic.

"You still there?" her sister said on the other end.

"Barely," Jenny said into the phone quietly. Her heart had finally started to beat again. "But I have to go. We'll talk later. Call me back."

Robert looked over his shoulder as he knelt down to the fireplace. "Tell her to call in the morning. I've got plans for tonight."

Jenny heard her sister squeal on the other end of the phone. "Plans! He's got plans!"

"He's talking about dinner." Jenny kept her voice even. She didn't want to encourage any rumors. "I think the plan is vegetable soup."

"For starters," Robert said as he lit a match to the log in the fireplace. "Only for starters."

Chapter Eleven

⌒❧

The next morning Jenny sat in the front seat of the four-wheel-drive Jeep Robert had borrowed from Linda and Duane at the café. Robert had promised her a surprise last night and this morning, after seeing that she could hobble along fine on her ankle, he told her might as well come and see it firsthand.

"This isn't the road to Billings." Jenny had steeled herself for the surprise. She didn't dare tell him that she could give him a surprise of her own.

How in the world had those tabloid editors put two and two together and come up with such an outlandish idea? Robert could very well be engaged. He could even be engaged to Laurel despite all his protesting. But one thing Jenny knew for sure was that he wasn't engaged to her.

She'd sorted through what her sister had told her

and decided Robert could be taking her to Billings to meet some mystery woman who was flying in to the airport there. That would explain the confusion in the tabloid editors' minds. Laurel must have said something about another woman. The fact that Jenny was one of only four single women in Dry Creek right now who were under seventy and over seventeen must have been what made the editors take such a leap of faith.

"Good thing it's not the road to Billings. We'd be stuck about now. Last I heard the road to Billings is closed. Too much drifting."

The sun shone a thin gray light down on the snow-packed road they'd taken out of Dry Creek. The air inside the Jeep was steamy warm, but the outside air had been heavy and damp. It could snow again anytime.

Jenny looked at Robert more closely. She wished the editors could see the man now. He didn't look like a man on his way to meet a woman he was planning to marry. There were no little twitches of repressed excitement. He hadn't even styled his hair. He'd combed it, but that was about it. Of course, that might just be because no one really styled their hair around here. Between the wind and the wool scarves, there were too many ways to mess it up.

"You never told me who owned Charlie." Jenny said cautiously. She wondered why she'd never considered that that old man in the desert might not have a daughter or a granddaughter or something. That would explain why Robert had spent five months there. He might have been doing more than chopping wood. Five months was plenty of time to fall in love.

"Charlie?" Robert looked over at her blankly. "I told you about Harry. He's the old man. Reminded me of Mr. Gossett who came to the lobster dinner the other night. He was hanging around the café the other day, too. Lonely, I suppose."

"The man you gave your coat to? The one the FBI is worried about—"

"Well, Mr. Gossett is more paranoid than Harry, but outside of that they're a lot alike. They live alone except for their pets. Harry has Charlie and I hear that old man Gossett has a whole bunch of cats. Feeds them real well from what I hear. Duane says it's mostly tuna—and not cat tuna, either. That's got to be quite a sacrifice on his Social Security income."

"So Harry lives alone." Jenny wondered if the sun wasn't suddenly shining a little warmer. "Just him and Charlie."

To the right of the road, Jenny could see the foothills of the Big Sheep Mountain range covered in a thick collar of snow. Snow hadn't collected on the sides of the mountains and they were a gray-brown. On each side of the narrow country road were wide ditches that caught the snow. Beside each ditch was a fence running along the road, dividing the grassland. The road rose and then dipped along with the low rolling countryside.

"At least this road looks usable," Jenny said. Things were looking up. All she had to do was screw up her courage and tell Robert about the latest engagement rumor. He knew all about the tabloids. He'd understand how a mistake like that could happen. All she had to do was tell him. Then they'd chuckle about the whole thing.

But not yet. She stalled. "Yes, the road is really all right."

Robert grunted. "If you don't count the bouncing."

Jenny felt the bumps in the road. She couldn't help it. The gravel road they were traveling over had obviously frozen solid after a muddy spell. The snow ahead filled in the ruts and made the road look smooth when it wasn't.

Thin lines of barbed-wire fence divided the various sections of land on each side of the road even though there were no cattle near the road.

"Makes me remember why I took up flying," Robert added as the Jeep bounced over another rut. "The ride's a lot smoother up in the sky."

"Speaking of flying, isn't your plane out this way?"

Robert turned to flash her a grin. "No questions. This is a surprise, remember."

"I thought you'd bring Mrs. Hargrove, too." Jenny unwrapped the wool scarf she'd wound around her head earlier.

Jenny should have told Robert about the rumors this morning at breakfast with Mrs. Hargrove and Laurel looking on. The older woman would have found a lesson in the absurd situation and afterward they wouldn't need to dwell on it. Laurel would have seen to that. She would turn the conversation back to herself as soon as possible. Yes, Jenny should have spoken up when the two of them were around.

Jenny added, "We should have brought Mrs. Hargrove. There's room in the Jeep for three people— even four. Laurel could have come, too. If it's some sort of rock formation or something, Laurel would like to see it."

"Laurel?" Robert snorted. "The only rocks she's interested in are the kind that slip on her finger. Besides, it's not a rock formation."

"Mrs. Hargrove says we're close to the Chalk Mountains. They have strange rock formations. She says the only things out this way are rocks and cattle."

The older woman had been excited that Robert was taking Jenny for a little drive with the promise of a surprise at the end of it. She'd bundled them both up and thrust a thermos of coffee into their hands early this morning before they'd started off.

"It's not a rock and it's not a cow. And Mrs. Hargrove doesn't know everything that's out here this morning."

Jenny revised her earlier opinion. Robert was beginning to look more and more like a man on his way to meet a special woman. His blue eyes were filled with anticipation. He looked boyish with his secret.

"So is it smaller than a bread box?" Jenny decided to play along.

Robert grinned. "I hope not. If it is, that means it got squashed."

"Bigger than a truck?"

"No."

"Is it a living thing?"

"Not at this moment."

Jenny considered a moment. "Would this thing interest the tabloids?"

Robert laughed. "You know, it just might at that. I'll have to ask your sister if she'd like to know the kind of gift I'm giving these days to impress a woman. That should convince them I'm not bachelor list material."

"I think they're already beginning to wonder about you being bachelor material."

"Really? You talked to your sister."

Here it goes, Jenny said to herself, as she took a deep breath. "Not this morning. It's from yesterday.

She told me their latest theory—seems they still think you're engaged.''

"I knew Laurel was talking to them.''

"Not to Laurel.''

"They know I'm not engaged to Laurel?'' Robert looked even more carefree than he already had been. "That's great!''

Jenny should speak now and finish the revelation. But she didn't. The road turned and she shifted on the seat. Then she looked out the side window and saw what was ahead. "What's your plane doing there? I thought it was back at Garth Elkton's ranch.''

Jenny remembered that plane well. She and Robert had flown from Seattle to Montana in it and landed it on a small road near Garth Elkton's ranch. The containers of lobster had filled up the back of the plane and she'd been strapped into the copilot's seat for the flight over. Robert had been preoccupied during the trip and she'd spent her time watching the instrument panel and wondering what all of the extra features were meant to do. She'd heard he had the instrument panel custom-made so he could include some high-tech gadgets.

"I moved the plane when you were napping yesterday. I needed to get it off the road. Besides, I needed it to be in a more open area. I'm using the homing device in it to coordinate with the plane that flew over.'' He turned to look at her. "You know, that's just great about the tabloids. Those guys are smarter than I gave them credit for being."

"Don't give them any credit yet."

Robert looked over at her. "Why not? They figured out Laurel was lying."

Jenny took another deep breath. She'd spit it out this time. "They think it's me."

"You?" Robert put his foot on the brake and turned to look at her. "What have you got to do with Laurel lying?"

"Not the lying." Jenny squared her shoulders and looked out the front window. The window was splattered with dirt. "They think it's me you're engaged to."

She couldn't see Robert, but the silence in the vehicle could only come from astonishment.

Jenny continued to study the dirt on the windshield. "My sister is young, you know, and really very romantic. Not that she told them we were engaged. I'm sure she'd never do that. But she might have mentioned the kisses—and, well, they're just so intent on having a story now that anything will do."

"Well, the old foxes," Robert said softly. "I'll never underestimate the tabloids again."

Jenny slipped a glance at him. He had eased up on the brake and was driving again. He looked happy. Maybe he hadn't understood.

"Hopefully they won't print their nonsense. I just

thought you should know. Of course, I've told my sister to tell them once again that it's not true. You're my employer and I'm just working a job here."

"You can't be working now." Robert started to whistle. "You don't have your hair net on."

Jenny's hands automatically went to her hair. "Well, I'm not working right now, of course, but—"

"Good," Robert interrupted her. "Because we're on a date."

Jenny gasped. "But we can't be on a date!"

"Granted, it's not a common date." Robert reached over and turned on the radio. Instrumental guitar music came from the small speakers on the front panel. "I wanted to get flowers, too, but we'll have to start with music. I had to call a station in Billings and beg them to play this stuff for us. Did you know that the guitar is one of the most romantic musical instruments ever played?"

"No." Jenny swallowed. Her hands were suddenly clammy. "No, I didn't know that."

"Some people hold out for the harp," Robert continued as he steered the Jeep to the side of the road and turned it to go down a small path that ran on the field side of a fence. "I've always found a harp to be almost too sweet for my taste. Reminds me of funerals. But maybe you like the harp. I don't think I'll find a radio station that even has it on file around here but I could patch it in from someplace else through my satellite connection on the plane. I get radio, phones and television from anywhere. Custom designed. I can get you harp if you like harp.''

"No, no, the guitar is fine.''

Jenny twisted the wool scarf she held in her hands. The man really must not have understood. "There's probably no need to worry. I'm sure the tabloids have to verify their facts before they print anything.''

Robert stopped whistling. "These are the tabloids! They print interviews with Big Foot!''

"Well, maybe they don't always verify. But space aliens can't sue. And I'm going to call my sister and tell them you'll sue them for everything they're worth if they print a story about you being engaged to—'' Jenny's throat closed, but she pushed the words out "—to me.''

"You want me to sue them?'' Robert's voice was quiet. "For saying we're engaged.''

Jenny glanced over at him. He was starting to frown. Good, she thought, he was finally beginning to understand. "Well, there won't be any need to sue if they just back off. I'm sure they're reasonable people and will understand it is in their best interests to not print such nonsense.''

"You think it's nonsense?''

"Well, it's not true.''

There was another moment of silence in the Jeep. Then Robert spoke. "It might not be true today, but who knows what might be true tomorrow."

Jenny's mind blanked. He couldn't be saying he'd consider—no, that was nonsense. If he was going to marry anyone, surely he'd pick someone like Laurel. Even the tabloids had. Jenny's mind stopped. Of course.

"I forgot that it would be convenient for you to be engaged to someone." Jenny's voice was small. "Even someone like me would stop the list. And I'm not like Laurel. I wouldn't be any trouble."

"Not any trouble?" Robert's voice was incredulous. "I can't even get you to date me. How do you figure you're no trouble?"

"Well, no one would know me." Jenny had helped her younger brothers and sisters get out of scrapes. She wondered if she'd be able to help this man, as well. "I mean, in your world, no one would know me. Your friends wouldn't be asking any awkward questions."

"I wouldn't count on it. I've found people always ask the awkward questions."

"Well, at least no one knows me except your mother. And you'll have to tell her the truth, so no one will be disappointed when the wedding doesn't come off."

"What about me? Maybe I would be disappointed."

No, Jenny thought to herself. She couldn't help this man get out of his trouble. "Fine. Be that way. If you're not going to take any of this seriously, you can just be on that list. It'll serve you right. Forget I even offered to help."

"I don't want you to pretend to be engaged to me."

Jenny blinked back a tear. "Of course not."

The Jeep stopped. Robert turned off the ignition. The radio stopped. The hum of the heater stopped.

"I just don't want to have any pretending between us," Robert said quietly.

Jenny nodded. She put her hands up again to feel her hair. The static from when she pulled the wool scarf off made her hair fly. She tried to press her hair down. She should have worn her hair net after all.

"Especially not to just feed the tabloids some story," Robert added. He opened the driver's door. "Now, if it was your sister doing the writing, that would be one thing."

"She'd never write about an engagement that wasn't true!"

A cold wind edged around the partially open driver's door. Robert turned to look at Jenny. "Then she should stick to selling pudding. Or move to another paper."

"She's just getting experience. It's not easy starting a career when you don't have connections."

"I know."

"She just needs a break."

Now this was the Jenny he knew. Her color had returned when she defended her younger sister. She no longer reached for a hair net that wasn't there. Her eyes flashed.

"We'll give her one."

Jenny looked up at Robert. He looked serious.

"The next big thing that happens, it's all hers," Robert declared. "And if nothing happens on its own, I'll make some news."

"Like what?"

"Maybe I could invite the Queen Mother to tea with a group of Elvis impersonators. Give your sister an exclusive press invitation."

"You know the Queen Mother?"

Robert nodded. "I even know the world's best Elvis impersonator. He's better than the King."

"And the Queen Mother would come if you invited her?" Jenny was stunned.

"Well, I'd probably need to rent a suite at some fancy London hotel—she doesn't travel much—but I could do that. Maybe invite the queen, too. Has your sister ever been to London?"

Jenny shook her head. She'd gone on a drive with a magician. What would he pull out of his hat next?

"Have you ever been to London?"

Jenny shook her head.

Robert nodded in satisfaction. "Good. Then it's settled. You and your sister will both come."

Robert liked the dazed look in Jenny's eyes. It had occurred to him last night that his surprise of boxes of food might disappoint her. He knew it would disappoint most of the other women he'd dated in his life. Now he knew he had London in his pocket just in case.

"To London? To meet the queen?"

"And the Queen Mother if you want." Robert congratulated himself. He was making progress.

Jenny looked at the dirt on the windshield again. What did one say to an invitation like that? "The guitar music was sweet. Thanks for arranging it."

Robert started to whistle. "My pleasure. And now for the other surprise—it's not much. But you need to let me come help you out of the Jeep before we go see it."

Robert fully opened the driver's door and stepped out. Jenny watched him walk around the front of the vehicle. That's when she noticed that the white outside was uneven. A wide piece of land had been scraped clean of snow. Probably yesterday. There was a dusting of white snow on it now, but the layers of snow that sat on the ground around it had all been scraped off the land and pushed to the side of an area. The scraped strip could be a runway for a plane.

The runway wasn't the only thing unusual beside

Robert's small plane. There was a large white tarp—
or maybe a parachute—that was draped over a
lumpy pile of what looked like boxes next to the
plane.

Robert opened Jenny's door with a bow. "The
surprise awaits. Permit me to help you down."

Jenny had borrowed an old pair of Mrs. Hargrove's snow boots this morning. Then Jenny had
pulled the bottoms of her gray sweatpants down over
the tops of the snow boots and she'd wrapped a very
old black wool jacket on before tying a beige scarf
around her head.

Jenny knew she looked fat as a snow bunny and
as uncoordinated as a church mouse. But Robert
looked up at her like she was royalty.

"The surprise is in the boxes," Robert said.

Jenny gave him her mittened hand and swung
around. "You didn't need to actually get me a surprise. I thought the surprise was something to look
at."

"Well, the first step is to look at the boxes," Robert pointed out as he helped her down from the Jeep.
"I had a pilot I know make a special drop for me."

In Robert's mind, he had planned to kiss Jenny
when she stepped out of the Jeep. But he didn't. She
was looking skittish and he didn't want to scare her
off.

The air was damp and heavy with the promise of

snow. Gray clouds hung in the sky. Jenny tightened the scarf around her neck.

Robert picked up one end of the parachute and pulled it off of the boxes. Ten industrial-size boxes stood in the middle of the tangle of cords. Two other smaller boxes were on one side of the pile.

Robert reached inside his coat for the pocket knife he'd brought. Those two smaller boxes might be the roses, he thought. He had only been able to leave a message with the pilot making the delivery. But the man must have added the roses at the last minute. Those two boxes sure didn't match the others.

"Let's start here." Robert ran his knife down the tape holding one of the smaller boxes together.

Robert had his mind on red roses and that was the only excuse he had for not looking at the box more closely. He'd opened the edge of the box, before he saw what it was. White lace started to spill out of the box. "That's not roses."

Jenny looked more closely at the box. A small tag was taped to the top of it. It was an airline baggage sticker that had been routed to the Billings airport.

Robert opened the box further. There were no roses hidden in the lace.

"That must be Laurel's dress," Jenny finally said. "The one she brought with her for the wedding."

"What the—" Robert looked into the box more closely. Jenny was right.

"The pilot must have stopped at the Billings airport."

"Well, she'll just have to take the dress back with her." Robert closed the flap on the box. "It was a fool stunt to bring one with her anyway."

"Would have been good for pictures, though." Jenny stepped closer to the boxes. The air was cold enough to make gray puffs around her when she breathed. She rubbed her hands together even in the mittens. "I've got to give her credit for thinking of that."

"Oh, Laurel can plan all right."

Robert looked over at Jenny. She was crouched down by the boxes. She was wrapped up in scarves and mittens. Her nose was red and her cheeks were white. What hair wasn't covered with a wool scarf fell every which way. She was adorable. "Wish I'd thought of pictures."

Jenny looked up at him. The sun fell on her and she smiled.

"I should have brought a camera with me. My mother probably still has one or two of those disposable ones," Robert said.

Jenny chuckled. "Not if those kids are around her. I heard two of them at the dance asking her for another camera. She said she'd given them all out. And no wonder, they way those kids were shooting pictures. Heaven only knows why they were taking so many pictures of us."

Robert didn't say anything. He and half of the Dry Creek population knew why the kids were taking pictures of him and Jenny. He was relieved that Jenny still didn't know.

"We'll just set Laurel's boxes aside." Robert pushed them to the side of the stack. "We've got some other boxes to open."

Chapter Twelve

"It's Romaine. The good kind." Jenny sat in the snow and hugged the lettuce. "You even had it packed in something so it would stay cold but wouldn't freeze. I can't wait. We'll have salad."

"With vine-ripened tomatoes," Robert couldn't help adding.

"And an avocado," Jenny added in supreme contentment. "Two avocados in fact."

Robert congratulated himself. He'd given women emeralds and rubies before and gotten less enthusiastic thanks.

"I'm sorry the roses didn't make it." The pilot had apparently not gotten the message Robert had left, but it didn't matter. Jenny was happy with her salad.

"And you have stuff for tacos. The kids will thank you."

Jenny forgave Robert any of his faults. He had thought of her and the kids, too. He'd remembered her craving for a romaine salad. Her sister was right. This man was special.

"I'm not so sure the kids are going to thank me. I've got some caviar stuck in those boxes someplace. My mother told me she wanted to expand the kids' horizons a little further. I'm not so sure about it myself. I think she might have pushed them to the limit with the lobsters. I told her she could tell the kids what she'd ordered for them." He shook his head. "I don't want to be responsible when they hear they have to eat caviar."

Jenny smiled. "The boys will love her."

Robert lifted an eyebrow. "You think?"

Jenny nodded. "They'll sneak the caviar off their plates and use it for ice fishing. After all, it's just fish eggs. I heard some of them worrying about what they could use for bait. They can't dig for worms in the frozen dirt around here."

"Fishing. Really? I think I have some fish hooks in my plane."

Robert stood up and held out a hand to Jenny as he continued. "Why don't we go see? Besides, it would be good to get out of the cold for a little bit and warm up. The plane has a heater I can turn on."

"You're sure you have enough fuel?"

"I have plenty of fuel. I could get back to Seattle and have some to spare."

The step into the plane was a high one, but once inside Jenny was glad she'd moved. The plane formed a cozy cocoon around the cockpit, partially because the sun shone in through the windows and heated the space enough so that it was very comfortable—especially if one was wrapped in wool like Jenny was.

To get to the cockpit, Jenny had needed to crawl through the small cargo space behind the pilot and copilot seats. When they left Seattle, that space had been filled with seafood boxes and boxes from Mrs. Buckwalter's house.

Jenny sat in the copilot seat. The windows were frosted around the edges, but she could see the Big Sheep Mountains straight ahead. A barbed-wire fence was to the left and open space was on the right. Everything was coated with snow.

"Is the heater on?" Jenny asked before she realized it was impossible. But there was a sound that made her think something was running.

Robert looked up. He heard the sound, too. "Someone's coming."

The two of them stood in the open space of the plane door and watched the pickup drive closer to them. Whoever was driving the pickup was doing a good job of it, but Robert felt a prickle of unease. Something was not right. There were three figures in the cab of the pickup and they were packed tight together. Which made sense. Then he saw it—

"Move back—" Robert swung his arm around to bring Jenny back into the shadow of the plane, but he was too late. He knew what had made him uneasy—that tall, skinny shadow in the window was a rifle.

A voice—Robert recognized the FBI agent's voice—called out. "Anybody home? You've got company. And trouble."

There wasn't room to maneuver and Jenny couldn't move too far. So Robert did the only thing he could. He stepped in front of her.

"Stay behind me," he whispered. *Dear Lord, don't let that gun go off.*

"What's wrong?"

"I don't know. Something with the FBI agent and that woman friend of his." Robert was looking out the plane door. The three figures got out of the pickup.

"Francis?"

"Uh-huh," Robert said as he raised his hands slowly until they were clearly in the open. "And our friend Mr. Gossett."

The old man didn't look drunk this morning. He did look a little crazy though. He was pointing that rifle of his at anyone and everyone. The barrel of it bounced around enough to show that the old man was nervous.

Robert had training in combating terrorist activity and knew an anxious criminal was the most dangerous kind. The old man walking toward him shouldn't be underestimated. Nor should his beat-up old rifle.

"Welcome." Robert schooled his voice to be calm as though nothing out of the ordinary was happening. Robert saw that the old man had a much newer pistol in his other hand as well as the rifle. "Nice day for a drive, isn't it?"

Robert noticed that Francis Elkton was wearing a dress and Flint Harris a suit. They huddled together as they walked closer to the plane with Mr. Gossett. They must have been on their way to church.

"Especially for a Sunday drive," Robert added as he leaned farther toward the opening in the plane. "Give me a minute to come down and I'll join you. Mrs. Hargrove packed us a thermos before we left. I'm sure there's enough coffee for five."

The thermos was the old-fashioned kind. It might do as a weapon. Or the diversion might be enough. With guns in both hands, however, the old man was dangerous. Robert waited until Jenny had reached the cockpit.

"Don't talk to me about Mrs. Hargrove," the old man grumbled. He stood in front of the open door on the plane. "Her and her Christian principles and then her not even willing to give me a ride to Billings today. I've been in her car plenty of times. I told her it was important and she doesn't listen to me. The woman just never listens. Worried about the snow, she says. What does she care if she gets stuck anyway? Someone would come looking for her in a blizzard. But me? No, nobody'll come for me. I had to stop them for a ride," Mr. Gossett pointed to Francis and Flint. "Mrs. Hargrove can go stew in her own coffee. I ain't drinking any of it."

"No problem. I won't pour a cup for you," Robert said easily as he held on to the side of the plane and swung down to the ground beside Mr. Gossett. "But maybe you don't mind if the rest of us have a cup."

The old man grunted. "Don't be too sure about that. I got me some business to get taken care of and I ain't got no time to waste on folks drinking coffee."

"Maybe Mr. Buckwalter has something stronger that you'd like instead," Francis suggested as she stepped into the circle. She looked at Robert, desperation edging her eyes. "Mr. Gossett is fond of his alcohol, you know."

"I could do with a beer," the old man admitted. "Should have brought me a couple. But I packed too fast."

No one remarked on the fact that the old man hadn't packed anything at all except for his rifle and the hat on his scrawny head. He hadn't even brought along much of a jacket.

"I don't have—" Robert wished he'd thought to put in some alcohol. He'd trade a whole ship full of the French-imported water that he had brought along right now for a pop-top can of the cheapest beer around.

"I saw some vanilla in those boxes," Jenny said as she showed herself again in the plane's door.

"I thought—" Robert started to scold Jenny as he turned to look up her.

Jenny lifted her chin and climbed to the ground. "It might be very good actually. It's a big bottle and would make quite a drink. Mrs. Buckwalter only buys pure vanilla—the beans have been soaking in alcohol for some time now."

"Well, goodness, girl, there's no reason to waste good alcohol on beans soaking it up," Mr. Gossett said as he used his rifle to gesture to Jenny. "Go get it for me. Me and your man here—" the old man pointed his gun at Robert "—we've got business to discuss in the meantime."

Robert smiled in relief. There for a second he thought the rifle barrel would follow Jenny. He shifted his position so it was even farther from the others. The rifle barrel followed.

"What can I do for you?" Robert asked politely, although he was almost certain he knew. The FBI was looking for the local informant who had tipped off the rustlers and, unless Robert missed his guess, the informant stood before him now as nervous as he deserved to be for betraying all the people of Dry Creek.

"I need me a plane ride."

Robert nodded like the request was reasonable. He kept his suspicions off his face and out of his voice. Let the man ask for what Robert knew he wanted. "Lots of people like to take a spin up in the air. I'd be happy to take you up for a few minutes." Robert turned and lightly slapped his hand against the side of his plane. "Nothing like a plane ride."

"A few minutes won't do it. I need to get me to another town. Maybe even across the border into Canada. I need to get out of Dry Creek one way or another. I'm what you might call a fugitive."

Well, the old man wasn't shy about laying his cards on the table. Robert took that as a good sign.

"The border won't work then." Robert calculated how long he could stall the old man. Robert looked up at the sky as though reading the signs of weather. "Not the best day for flying, either. Gusty winds. A blizzard could blow up. You wouldn't want to be in the air then. Maybe you'd be better off going tomorrow instead. I could drive you somewhere tomorrow personally. Keep your feet on the ground that way."

The old man snorted. "By tomorrow I'll be arrested and my feet won't care where they are. I think I'll take my chances with getting to Canada."

"Canada?" Robert stalled. "I don't know."

"That's where people always run to," the old man persisted stubbornly. "They say they're going across the border and they do. That's where I'm going."

"That's the Mexican border they're talking about," Robert confirmed patiently as he shifted his feet again. He wanted to keep the old man's attention, and Robert figured the best was to do that was to fidget enough to keep the rifle focused on him. "But I don't have enough fuel to fly that far. And there's no point in flying across the Canadian border. There might be more paperwork to ship you back, but they'd do it all the same. You wouldn't be solving any problems that way."

"I don't want to go to jail," the old man said stubbornly. "I can't stand them small cells they have."

"Claustrophobic, huh?"

"Clausta' who?" Mr. Gossett squinted at Robert. "No need to get fancy in the word department. It was only cows missing anyway. Not like anyone around here was killed or anything."

Robert bit his tongue before he could remind the old man that Glory Beckett had almost died because of the rustling business the old man had treated so lightly. The fact that no one had died yet was only because of God's grace. The old man in front of him surely couldn't take any credit for that.

"The plane's got enough fuel to fly to someplace like Fargo, North Dakota, or we could head into Billings if you'd like." Robert said the destinations clearly and turned so his voice would carry clearly to the others. If he was flying anyone anywhere he wanted it to be only one or two choices and for those choices to be heard by everyone around.

"I'll take Fargo. Let's all get inside."

"You don't mean everyone, I'm sure." Robert was sure of no such thing, but he nodded calmly and then added as an afterthought, "Taking everyone will slow us down. Plus, the fuel will last longer if the plane is lighter." Robert measured the old man with his eyes. "I'd say you're about one hundred seventy pounds?"

Mr. Gossett nodded.

"I'll go with you to fly this thing, but you don't need the others."

The old man pondered a moment. "I'll need a hostage."

"That would be me," the FBI agent stepped forward.

Robert nodded slightly. Yes, if Flint and he got Mr. Gossett up in the air, they could handle him.

The old man snorted. "I don't think so. I'll take her." He jerked his head at Jenny who was just returning with a large bottle of vanilla in her hand. "She's a skinny little thing. Can't weigh much."

"You don't need her," Robert protested. "I've got fuel enough to fly three men."

"It's not just about weight," the FBI agent added. "In case something goes wrong, I can talk to the authorities for you."

"Nothing had better go wrong."

The agent shrugged. "You never know."

"You speak fancy enough, don't you?" the old man demanded of Jenny as he held out his hand for the vanilla bottle.

Silently Jenny gave him the bottle as she shrugged.

"Well, it doesn't need to be all that fancy. She can talk for me," Mr. Gossett insisted as he slipped the bottle into the pocket of his coat. "Now, you two men see that all of the boxes are out of that plane. I don't want any unnecessary weight holding us back."

Robert's heart sank. He had hoped the old man would tip the vanilla bottle back the minute he got it. That would give them their one good chance to get that rifle away from him.

"Jenny's heavier than she looks," Robert offered easily.

Jenny started to sputter then realized what Robert was doing. "I guess I am pretty heavy. We burned a lot of fuel flying in from Seattle."

Mr. Gossett snorted and pointed his rifle directly at Jenny. "Don't start giving me trouble now. I'm the one who says who is going and you're going 'cause I say you're going.''

"Of course," Jenny said softly.

"She's not going," Robert said flatly as he turned his body so he could shield Jenny if the old man swung that rifle around again. *Please, God, help me on this one. I'll go. I'll go gladly. But not Jenny.*

"An' why not?" the old man reared up and demanded.

"The plane won't fly with her in it." Robert said the words in his most authoritative voice hoping the nonsense would pass for truth. "We almost didn't make it into Dry Creek. Had to crash-land over by the Elkton place. Something to do with the instrument panel. One of those energy things related to chemicals in the body. Makes the instruments go haywire. Something to do with energy fields or hormones, maybe both."

The old man snorted, but Robert could see that he wasn't sure.

"Well, if she doesn't go, she hits the ground with the two of them," Mr. Gossett finally said.

The ground would work, Robert thought to himself. Jenny would get a little snow on herself that she'd have to brush off when the plane left, but the ground would be safer than the air.

"You two—get down on the ground." The old man jerked his gun at Francis and Flint.

"What?" the FBI agent questioned.

Robert could see that the agent was trying to move behind the old man, but there was no way.

"It's just that the ground is frozen." Robert stepped in. "Let them at least go sit in the pickup— or even the Jeep. There's no way they can catch us in a Jeep once we're in the air."

Robert was starting to breathe again. Jenny would be even better in the Jeep. The heater would keep them warm and they could drive back into Dry Creek and get help. The sheriff would call over to the airports at Billings and Fargo and let them know what was happening.

"The ground. Now," the old man insisted. "I don't have all day. I gotta get out of here."

Francis lowered herself to the ground. The snow was not yet packed down and she sank into the few inches that covered the place where the snow had been scraped off earlier.

"You, too," the old man ordered Flint. "I want you with your back to her—" the old man shifted his gaze to Jenny "—and you get some rope from those boxes to tie them up."

"You're not going to leave them like that?" Robert protested. He hadn't counted on the people on the ground being tied up. That changed everything. If they were tied, they needed to be someplace warmer. "Why not just tie them up in one of the vehicles?"

Robert hadn't lived in Montana. He didn't know

about the winters here. But it didn't take much knowledge of weather to realize that the two people before him could freeze to death if they were tied up out here in the open.

"What does it matter to me if they get cold?" the old man snarled. "That'll teach them to come snooping around, asking questions. Butting into a man's private life. Looking through his trash cans."

The old man kept the rifle pointed at Jenny the whole time he ordered her to tie up Francis and Flint and then he walked with her over to the two vehicles and ordered her to pull out some wires and give them to him.

Robert didn't remind the old man that there had been any suggestion that Jenny wait with the other two on the ground instead of joining them in the air. He could tell by the expression on the FBI agent's face that the ground could be a death sentence. At least if Robert had Jenny with him in the plane, he could call some of the shots. The old man wouldn't know how to fly a plane. He would need Robert's cooperation.

Robert kept reminding the old man that a plane did not fly itself the whole time the three of them were preparing to take off from the makeshift runway on that cow pasture just north of Dry Creek.

"You can put the gun away," Robert repeated. He had started the engines and was checking out the instrument panel. "No one's going to sneak up on you when you're inside here."

The old man was crouched in the baggage compartment of the plane. Jenny was strapped into the copilot's seat and Robert was in his own place. The man had kept the rifle pointed at Jenny.

The sound of the engine was a constant background noise as Robert maneuvered the small plane for takeoff.

Robert was almost ready to turn around to begin the take off when they all heard it.

The cell phone was ringing.

Robert looked at Jenny. The cell phone was in the pocket of her parka. "Let it ring."

The old man shifted the rifle in his hands. "Give it to me. I'll decide who answers what."

Jenny nodded as she reached into her pocket and pulled out the small black phone. "It's probably just a wrong number."

The old man grunted as he took the phone and looked at it. The phone rang again in his hand and he studied the phone for a moment before he pressed the button to receive the call. "Hello?"

Chapter Thirteen

Jenny held her breath as though she could will her sister to hang up when she heard a strange man's voice. *Lord, let her know it's trouble.*

"Yes," Mr. Gossett answered hesitantly. "He's here, but he's busy."

Jenny looked over at Robert. He was glancing back at Mr. Gossett by looking at the old man's reflection in the instrument panel. It was close to freezing inside the cockpit of the small plane and yet Robert had a thin sheen of sweat on his forehead.

Jenny felt the coldness in her bones one minute and she flashed hot the next. The shoulder strap of the seat belt dug into her arm when she turned to look at Mr. Gossett.

The old man was concentrating on the phone, but he still had the rifle angled at Jenny. He frowned like he was arguing with someone. "Can't it wait? He's busy right now."

Robert moved his hand slightly to turn one of the knobs on the instrument panel. He looked over at Jenny. "I'm sorry I got you into this."

"You?" Jenny looked at him in astonishment. "What did you do?"

"If I wasn't so intent on impressing you with the fact that I could give you anything, we wouldn't have been out at the plane this morning. We would have been in church like Mrs. Hargrove would want."

"Mrs. Hargrove thought it was great that you were giving me a surprise."

"She thought I was going to show you a rock."

"Well, still—you couldn't have known what would happen."

The old man interrupted their conversation by thrusting the black cell phone up front. "This woman says she needs to talk to you—claims she's a saleswoman for some big pudding company. I've been trying to tell her you're busy."

Robert looked over at Jenny as he took the phone from the old man.

"Hello, Robert Buckwalter speaking." Robert put the phone to his ear.

Jenny hoped her sister would take the hint from the formality in Robert's voice that they were in a serious situation.

Jenny twisted her neck so she could look back at the old man. She'd hoped he'd relaxed some. He hadn't. He had the rifle angled toward her and his eyes were suspicious.

"Sorry about the phone call," Jenny said. She kept her voice calm and low. She thought that if she talked to the old man it would mask any conversation Robert was having with her sister. Maybe he could slip her a hint about their situation.

"Fool things—them portable phones."

"Yes, I suppose they are," Jenny agreed.

Jenny heard Robert talking about an order for chocolate pudding. Apparently the old man did as well because he relaxed somewhat.

"Those salesmen—they'll find you anyplace you go," the old man grumbled. "There's no peace anywhere."

"It does seem that way." Jenny wondered what salesmen had had the nerve to call at Mr. Gossett's home.

"That's what's wrong with the world—all this buy, buy, buy…" The old man's voice trailed off.

"No, I can't place an order now. I'm getting ready to fly my plane—delicate cargo." Robert's conversation filled in the gap in the old man's complaining.

"Did you need more money?" Jenny frantically tried to keep her conversation with the old man alive so that he would not be listening to Robert just in case Robert was fool enough to mention anything concrete about the danger they were in.

"Me?" Mr. Gossett seemed startled. "Why would I need more money?"

The old man was starting to look at Robert suspiciously. At the moment, Robert was talking about the number of calories in a cup of pudding.

"But then why did you do it?" Jenny knew it was a gamble, but the question pulled the old man's attention back to her. She hoped her sister could decode whatever message Robert was giving her. "The rustling. Why did you tip them off about the cattle?"

"Dry Creek owed it to me," Mr. Gossett said. "They owed it to my family. My father founded Dry Creek, you know. Wouldn't be no town without him."

"You must have been very proud."

"I wasn't proud. I wasn't nothing," the old man grumbled, and then turned to Robert. "You're done talking to that saleswoman. It's time for us to get out of here."

"Yes, the delivery is important," Robert said into the phone. "I expect the pudding to be there when I arrive at two o'clock."

"An' I expect you to hang up when I say hang up," the old man said nastily.

Robert put the phone into a cradle in the instrument panel. Jenny was surprised. She hadn't realized it was the plane's cell phone they had been using since their arrival in Dry Creek.

"The pudding will be ready when we get there," Robert said to Jenny quietly as he adjusted a few knobs on the instrument panel.

"Ah—" Jenny gave a small barely audible gasp when she saw that the cell phone's light was still lit. The phone was still on. Her sister could still hear everything. Jenny quickly coughed to cover her slip.

Now that Jenny thought about it, Robert had received a phone call when they were flying in from Seattle. He had explained that he had some kind of satellite reception capability in the plane's system. No wonder that cell phone worked in Dry Creek when her own personal one didn't.

"You sure do set an unnatural store by that pudding of yours," the old man grumbled. "In my day, we used to make our own pudding. Real milk and cream. Butter. Flour. None of this prepackaged stuff they feed you today."

"We're ready for takeoff," Robert said and then looked toward the back of the plane. "You might want to lay your rifle down, Mr. Gossett, for the ascent portion of the takeoff. Change in cabin pressure and everything. Jenny here's going to start feeling like she's your hostage."

"She is my hostage—thought I said that before," the old man insisted.

"Well, it's a long ride to Fargo," Robert continued easily. "No point in having your rifle out all that time. Nobody here's going anywhere until we land this plane at the airport there anyway."

"Thanks, but I'll keep the rifle ready if you don't mind. I don't aim to be no fool."

"Of course not," Robert agreed easily as he started to move the levers and buttons on his panel. Several clicks followed each other.

"Not that I'm not thankful that you haven't shot your rifle at anyone," Jenny clarified for her sister. She wanted her sister to alert the authorities, but not worry their mother.

Robert grunted a warning. Jenny knew the warning was for her although she suspected Mr. Gossett might think it was for him. She was right.

"I aim to be comfortable on this trip," the old man said defiantly. "That means keeping my rifle pointed where I want it pointed."

"Of course," Robert said smoothly.

Jenny felt the small plane start to rise.

The plane rose in the air gracefully. They were up a hundred feet when Robert banked slightly as though waving to the two people on the ground. Jenny looked down and watched the figures of Flint and Francis grow smaller.

Be with them, Father. Jenny prayed. *Send them someone. And in the meantime, keep them warm.*

If it had been another morning, Jenny would revel in the plane flight. Robert rose high enough that they were flying just under the gray clouds. It was like flying through the underside of a cotton ball. Strings of gray swirled around the plane, but visibility was never gone.

"At least we have heat up here," Robert said as he pushed a lever and the flow of warm air increased. Robert turned his neck slightly so he could see the old man in the cargo area. "Warm enough for you back there?"

The old man snorted. "You can't fool me."

Jenny's heart froze. The old man must suspect the telephone was still working.

"You've got plenty of heat," the old man continued talking. "I see it on the gauge there. No need to be skimpy with the heat. Don't let it hang down there at sixty degrees. Crank it up. Remember us old folks feel the cold more than you young ones. And don't be thinking you can pull anything over on me. I'm watching."

"Of course," Robert said once again. "Just sit back and pretend you don't have anything to worry about."

The old man snorted. "Got me plenty to worry about. I've figured that one out."

"If any of your troubles are related to money, I've got plenty that you're welcome to have if we get landed safe and sound." Robert had seldom laid down such an obvious bribe.

"Don't tell him you're rich," Jenny whispered softly. "He'll keep us for ransom."

Robert laughed. "I think he already knows by now I'm rich. Not many poor people have their own planes."

"Yeah, that ransom bit though, that's not a bad idea," the old man said gleefully from the back of the plane. "I had to leave all the money I got from those rustlers back home. Didn't have time to dig it up now that the ground's frozen."

"You had it buried!" Jenny turned around to look at the old man. He was huddled against the wall of the plane, hugging the barrel of his rifle. "Why?"

"You never know who's watching," he said indignantly. "I didn't want one of my neighbors to rob me!"

"Robbed in Dry Creek? By who?"

"I've got my enemies there. You can be sure. But you youngsters wouldn't know about things like that. How everything gets tangled up when you live with the same folks for seventy-some years," the old man said stubbornly.

"But surely they wouldn't rob you."

"They would if they could. But I'm too smart for them. I know how to take care of my money." The old man took a deep breath. "And I'll be thinking of what money I'll need for a ransom for our friend here." Mr. Gossett jerked his head toward Robert. "Being a rich man, he'll be worth a penny or two."

"And Jenny, too." Robert looked into the rearview mirror, which showed him the back of the plane. "I'll pay a good amount for her, too."

Robert could see the protest grow on Jenny's face, but he continued. "My only condition is the obvious one."

"What?" the old man demanded.

"We need to both be safe and free. She and I— we're together in this. You hurt her, you've hurt me. If you're going to hurt anyone, it's me. If you harm a single hair on her head, the only thing you get from me is a lifetime of trouble."

The old man grunted. "You lovebirds. If I'd have known it was like that, I'd have brought the FBI agent instead."

The air inside the small plane was overly warm now. Jenny felt sweat in her palms. "We're not lovebirds."

The old man grunted. "Don't make me no never mind if you are. I was young once. I know what it's like to love someone." He focused on the back of Robert's neck. "How much money you figure your lady friend here is worth?"

"You're welcome to every penny I have if you keep her safe."

"Don't suppose you know what time it is?" the old man said suddenly, and leaned forward to look at the instrument panel. "Hey, what are all those gadgets?"

Jenny scrambled for something to say. She didn't know if Mr. Gossett would realize the significance of that little red light on the cell phone or not.

"I thought you said you didn't help the rustlers because of the money," Jenny reminded the man boldly.

Her distraction worked. He reared back from his squatting position indignantly. "I always believe in getting my due from people—and Dry Creek owed me and my family. It was time they paid and paid up good."

Robert made some adjustments to the altitude. Not much, but it would be enough to make the old man sit back down.

"Sorry," Robert said smoothly as the plane dipped a little. "Must be some turbulence. It'd be a good idea to slip one of those seat belts on back there. Keep you from bouncing around."

"There wasn't much wind earlier," Mr. Gossett said suspiciously.

"From the looks of it, there's a blizzard coming in," Robert cautioned the man. He didn't add that the blizzard appeared to be twenty hours away. They'd be safely landed somewhere by then. He only had fuel left for four hours.

"But where will I go in a blizzard?" Mr. Gossett asked quietly from the back seat. He had belted himself into one of the side seats. "I can't go back home."

"I'm sure there's a hotel," Jenny comforted the man. "Just ask the desk at the airport. They'll tell you how to get a cab to a hotel."

"I've never been to a big city before."

"Fargo's not that big," Robert stated clearly. "You'll see when we fly within range of it in an hour and—" Robert looked down at his watch "—thirty-five minutes. And, oh, by the way, my watch reads one-fifteen."

"Mrs. Hargrove would have brought my Sunday plate over by now," the old man mumbled wearily. "Probably that meat loaf of hers. I love that meat loaf. And maybe some mashed potatoes."

"She's been a good neighbor to you."

The old man grunted. "That's all you know about it."

"Well, I don't know what else she could have done." Jenny wanted to keep Mr. Gossett a little upset so he didn't pay too much attention to the red light on the cell phone as it jutted out of the instrument panel.

"That's just it," Mr. Gossett said emphatically. "You don't know. Nobody knows, not even Helen herself."

"Helen?"

"Mrs. Hargrove to you. Used to be Helen Boone." The old man's voice softened. "She used to be the prettiest thing when she was Helen Boone.

I used to leave flowers on her desk at school some mornings.''

"Isn't that nice.'' Jenny was hoping for some common ground. "I didn't know you used to be sweet on her.''

"Me?'' The old man sounded startled. "I never said that. I never said that to anyone. Not ever.''

"But you left her flowers.'' Jenny turned around so she could see the man clearly even though he was no longer looking ahead at her.

Mr. Gossett grunted. "For all the good it done me. She thought it was Frank Hargrove leaving them.''

"And you never told her.''

The old man shrugged. "Thought she should have known it was me leaving the flowers. So I was stubborn. Next thing I knew Frank Hargrove up and asked her to marry him and she said yes. It was too late then. They were beholden and I knew Helen wouldn't go back on her word.''

"So you've loved her in silence all those years?''

The old man didn't move for a moment and then he finally said, "Didn't seem to be much I could do about it.''

"But to not even tell her.''

The wrinkles on the old man's face seemed to fold into him, but he didn't answer the question. Of course, Jenny thought to herself, what could he say? He'd not even had the courage to tell the woman he loved how he felt. Instead, he'd let his love sour him until he became a bitter old recluse.

"I don't suppose you've been to Fargo?" Robert cut into the silence with a question for Jenny.

Jenny looked over at him. He obviously wanted the talk to continue so that her sister, or by now probably the police, could monitor them.

"There was a movie by that name," Jenny offered. "But I missed it."

"It'll be small-town America at its best," Robert added as he shifted in his seat to look in the mirror that allowed him to see where Mr. Gossett sat. He called back to the man. "Feel free to take a nap if you'd like."

The old man grunted and sat up straighter. "Don't take me for no fool."

"Of course not," Robert replied smoothly. "Just want you to be comfortable."

"I can be comfortable when I'm back home in my bed."

"Back in Dry Creek?" Robert asked in surprise.

Jenny looked at Mr. Gossett and said softly, "We're headed to Fargo."

"Yeah." The old man nodded wearily. "I'm gonna miss that old bed at home."

Jenny did her best to bring up conversation topics. She went through stories of her growing-up years. She talked about her favorite recipes. She recited a favorite poem. Robert would answer here and there, but mostly he just sent her thankful glances. By now the plane was encountering some real turbulence and he had to watch the instrument panel closely.

Jenny periodically glanced over her shoulder to see if Mr. Gossett had nodded off yet. She didn't quite know how they would manage, but she knew that she or Robert would need to try and take the rifle from the old man if he fell asleep.

The air inside the plane was warm and Jenny had been talking for over an hour. She had almost forgotten the reason why she was talking.

And then it happened—

From the other end of the cell phone came the distinct sound of a sneeze.

The old man sat up straight. "What was that?"

Jenny's heart stopped. She looked at Robert.

"I sneezed," Robert said easily. "Must be coming down with something."

There was silence for a moment and Jenny started to relax.

"No, you didn't," the old man finally said. "That sneeze was too far away—besides, it was a woman's sneeze."

Jenny resisted the urge to say that the sneeze was hers. She knew the old man had been able to see her clearly all along and he would know she was lying.

The old man leaned forward so he could put his

head between Jenny and Robert and look at the instrument panel clearly.

"That phone's still on," the old man announced. "That pudding person's still listening."

Jenny shivered. The old man who had talked about his young love was gone. The man who sat behind them now was a hard man. And he had a rifle in his hands.

Jenny felt the round cold circle of the rifle barrel pressed against the side of her head.

"I don't like being double-crossed," Mr. Gossett said. "I don't like it at all."

Robert positioned the plane so it would fly as smooth as possible without him.

"I'm the one who left the phone on," Robert said. "Threaten me if you're going to threaten anyone."

The old man laughed. Robert felt his heart constrict. There was no amusement in the laughter. The old man no longer sounded pathetic. He sounded dangerous.

"I'm not going to threaten," the old man announced wearily as he slowly cocked the rifle. "I'm tired of people not treating me right."

"You can't blame Jenny for Dry Creek," Robert said as he unhooked his seat belt so he could move. "What happened there happened many years ago."

Lord, keep him talking, Robert begged.

"And Robert—he gave you his coat," Jenny added.

The old man grunted. "It's all too late."

"Put that rifle down." Robert tried again. "If you don't, I won't fly you to Fargo. I'll set us down right here. Look down—it's nothing but white. We'll all freeze to death."

"I don't much care where I die. But I do figure that I may as well get even before I go."

"Hurting Jenny won't make you even." Robert moved everything so he could twist and tackle the man in one smooth movement. Robert knew he'd have to be quick about it.

"I suppose you'll be lonesome without her," the old man turned to Robert and snarled. "Just like I was—all those years alone."

"As a matter of fact, I would be lonesome without her," Robert said softly. "I can't imagine living the rest of my life without her."

Jenny had watched Robert move around so that he was free of all the belts and the levers keeping him in the pilot seat.

"Now I lay me down to sleep." Jenny started to pray the old prayer she and her sister had prayed as little girls. Then thinking of the sneeze that might have come from her sister, she added, "No matter what happens here today, I want everyone to know it's no one's fault."

The old man grunted in protest. "It's the fault of someone."

"Who?" Jenny asked. The barrel of the rifle no longer pressed so hard against her head. She wasn't sure if that was a sign of hope or a sign of doom.

The old man was silent for a moment before he whispered, "Helen. It's her fault. She should have known."

Mr. Gossett might have had a tear in his eye. Robert believed that he did and that was why, when Robert swung back and tackled him, the old man just seemed to crumble. Taking the rifle away was not even difficult.

Robert reached for a length of rope that had been tied around some boxes on the trip out from Seattle and handed it to Jenny. "Can you tie him up?"

Jenny nodded as she slid past Robert on his way back to the pilot's seat.

The old man sat in silence for the ten minutes it took them to reach the Fargo airport. Jenny spent the first five minutes of the ten speaking into the cell phone and reassuring her sister that everything was fine. The final five minutes Jenny spent wondering why Robert was so quiet.

"What's that?" Jenny said as she looked out the window.

It was the middle of the afternoon and the land all around the runway was blanketed with white snow and ice. But a crowd lined the runway anyway.

There must have been a dozen vans with block letters on their doors and shiny reflectors on their top.

"What's happening—a parade?" Jenny asked.

"Not quite," Robert said. "Those are television crews getting their lights set up for interviews."

"Interviews? With who?"

Robert grimaced. "Us."

Chapter Fourteen

Jenny's throat was sore and her face was tired. She had never before smiled until the muscles in her face hurt. And her eyes! Her eyes burned from being in the flash of a hundred camera shots.

She was a wreck.

"No, it was Mr. Gossett who said that—the gunman," Jenny repeated for the tenth time. Or was it the twentieth? "Robert Buckwalter and I are not lovebirds. He is my employer's son. I'm the chef."

"Then why was he willing to ransom you even if it took every penny he had?" a reporter called from the back line. "You must be some cook."

"Miss Black is refusing to answer any questions about ransom and so am I." Robert came out of the room where he had been talking with the police. "And if you have a shred of decency, you won't print that remark in any of your papers." Robert stopped to eye the reporters sternly. "A remark like that would set Miss Black up as a kidnapping target and you know it."

"Kidnapping? Me?" Jenny blinked. She'd never given much thought to the problems of a rich family, but she was beginning to see that there were many. Even though the arrest of Mr. Gossett would have stirred up some news by itself, the number of reporters at the Fargo airport would have been reduced by almost ninety percent if the Buckwalter family hadn't been involved in the story. Only a few of the reporters had even bothered to take a picture of the old man being arrested by the police when he walked off the plane.

"So it was just the old man talking," a woman reporter called out. "There really is no secret engagement?"

Robert looked at Jenny. She looked scared and a little bewildered. She'd had enough pressure for one day. He turned and formally addressed the group. "No, there's no secret engagement. Now, excuse us, we've had a long day."

The reporters gave a unified sigh of disappointment.

"But won't you give one of us an exclusive on the story?" one reporter called out as he waved his arm. "I volunteer."

All of the other arms started to wave.

"Sorry, but the exclusive is already spoken for," Robert said as he guided Jenny out of the spotlight from the cameras.

Two airport security staff flanked Robert and Jenny as they walked away from the reporters.

"Sorry about that," Robert said to Jenny as he steered her quickly into the office of some airport official. "I thought they were going to put you in a locked office, too."

"I had to leave to use the rest room."

Robert nodded. "Oh, well. They might have found you anyway. But don't worry. It'll be over soon. The plane I've ordered will be here in fifteen minutes or so. It'll take you home."

"Oh, we're going back to Dry Creek?"

Robert looked at her strangely. "I thought you might want to visit your mother in Seattle for a few days, so I arranged for a pilot friend to fly you there. You can get your ankle checked out better, too."

Jenny looked down at her foot. "It's fine. It hasn't hurt all day."

"Still, it should be X-rayed. And you'll want to rest."

"Rest?"

Jenny was speechless. She was being sent home like she was some pet that had suddenly become inconvenient. She had come to believe that Robert was not like that kind of rich person. She had come to believe he was different. She had come to believe he was— Jenny stopped herself and then silently admitted the truth—she had come to believe he was the one and only one for her.

No wonder he was sending her home.

"I'll ask someone to pack the suitcase I have in Dry Creek and send it back, as well." Jenny walked stiffly to the door.

Robert almost lost his courage. He'd hoped she would refuse to go away for even a minute. He knew she'd be a target for every tabloid reporter in the country if she stayed in Fargo tonight or went back to Dry Creek with him tomorrow, and yet he could hardly bear for her to go.

"I don't think the press will find you in Seattle." Robert handed her a folded piece of paper, "But if they do call, tell your mother to have them call this number. I'll come to see you in a few days and we'll talk."

Sure, Jenny thought, and all those owners who dumped off their pets in the abandoned lot were really only going for a little drive to the store before they came back to pick up their beloved kittens.

But what had she expected? He was richer than King Midas. And she was the cook. He had more millions in the bank than she had spoons in the kitchen.

Suddenly Jenny wanted very much to see her own family for a few days.

"There's the plane now," Robert said softly as

he bent down and kissed the top of her head. "I'll see you soon. Very soon."

"Sure." Jenny didn't look back as she walked out the door.

The weather in Seattle was cold and damp. Gray clouds seemed to be all there was to the sky. Jenny's mother had welcomed her home with a tight hug. Her mother had already heard a news report of what had happened.

The first day Jenny was home she slept for twelve hours. The next day she slept for ten. On the third day her mother's fussing started to turn to alarm and so Jenny got up.

"You've been working too hard," her mother said when Jenny padded out into the living room in stretched-out sweatpants that had been left behind by one of her sisters. "Those dinners you give—there's a lot of hard work in doing them. And, if that's not bad enough, you have to go up in an airplane with some gunman."

"Mr. Gossett wasn't your usual gunman," Jenny protested. As the days passed, she'd felt more and more sorry for the old man. He'd looked so defeated when he was arrested. "I'm not sure if he'd have ever actually pulled that trigger."

The latest report said Mr. Gossett had turned state's evidence and worked with the FBI to arrest the major criminals in the rustling ring.

Jenny's mother snorted. "Well, I'm glad your Robert didn't wait around to find out if the old man was going to shoot you or not. At least he showed some sense."

"He's not my Robert." Jenny had made the protest already a dozen times since her mother had first heard the story.

"That's not what it said on television yesterday."

"Television? What was on television?"

"It was yesterday afternoon—I can't remember the name of the show—it has that cute man as a host. Anyway, he interviewed someone who had heard the telephone tape of what had happened in the plane—and the witness said that you were Robert's new girlfriend."

"It's not true," Jenny said patiently. She wanted to wrap herself in hair nets and shapeless sweatpants. "It was only the old man talking. And he was half-crazy."

Jenny wanted nothing more than to go back to sleep. She figured this media frenzy was like a virus. If you just went to bed, it would all go away in a few days.

"You need to get dressed." Jenny's mother eyed her critically. "Put on something cheerful. What if someone comes?"

"No one is going to come—" Jenny stopped and eyed her mother suspiciously. "You haven't gotten any phone calls, have you? You know that if a reporter calls, you're to ask them to call that number I gave you."

Jenny's mother drew herself up. "The man assured me he's not one of those reporters. He just has a question."

The phone in the kitchen rang.

"I'll get that," Jenny's mother said. "You go get changed."

Jenny went into her old room and stared into the nearly empty closet. She had only a few clothes left from the days when she lived here with her mother. The best of the lot was an emerald-green linen dress. But that would require nylons, she supposed, and she didn't want a reporter to think that she had dressed up just to tell him to leave.

Jenny knew there was only one logical question for the reporter to ask. It was the question everyone else was asking—was she Robert Buckwalter's new girlfriend?

Jenny grimaced at herself in the mirror. The best way to answer that question was to stay in these old sweats. No one would even think to ask if she was some rich man's girlfriend then.

"Are you dressed?" Jenny's mother called from the kitchen. "Your sister wants to talk to you."

"I'll be there in a minute." Jenny slipped the sweatshirt off and the linen dress on. She'd forgo the nylons.

Jenny brushed her hair on the way to the kitchen.

Jenny's mother gave her the phone.

"I can't get any pictures," her sister wailed the minute Jenny put the phone to her ear. "I got some really good quotes from Robert about you and he cooking that lobster dinner, but the editor wants pictures."

"Well, surely someone has pictures," Jenny said. So Robert had kept his word and fed the story to her sister. "I wish I had some, but I don't. I'm sure someone does, though. There were more of those little disposable cameras at that dinner than there were salt shakers."

"I know. But no one's selling."

"Why not? Oh, of course. The kids think they are being loyal by not dealing with the press."

"I don't know about that. They're sure dealing with someone," her sister said. "I've offered a couple of them five hundred dollars for a shot of you and Robert dancing, but they won't sell—they tell me they have an offer for a thousand dollars minimum."

"What? Who would pay that for those pictures? Besides, those kids took dozens of pictures. Surely someone will sell one of theirs."

"I asked around," Jenny's sister said quietly. "Apparently all of the pictures are spoken for."

"And someone's paying a thousand dollars for each one! That's amazing! Are you sure the kids aren't just trying to jack the price up?"

"They did jack the price up," her sister protested. "I finally just asked one of them to name their price—and they said that it wasn't for sale. They said someone would pay a hundred dollars more than any offer I made."

"What kind of a fool would do that?"

There was a long pause. "I think it's Robert."

"But why would he do that?" Jenny protested. "Surely he doesn't really want all those pictures."

Then it hit Jenny. Robert may not want the pictures, but he wanted even less for the media to have them.

"I was wondering if you could talk to him for me," Jenny's sister asked hesitantly. "I mean you still work for him—"

"—for his mother." Mrs. Buckwalter had called and left a message that Jenny was to consider herself on a paid vacation for the week she was spending with her mother.

"Well, could you ask? I've tried to reach him on the phone, but he's not answering. I think he'd throw a picture my way if he remembered I need one to feature my story. He was so nice. He called me and actually suggested we do this interview. My editor was so impressed. The only thing Robert wouldn't talk about was that lovebird remark the old man made."

"He's worried people will believe it."

"Well, of course they'll believe it if they read

about it,'' Jenny's sister said cheerfully. "How do you think progress gets made?''

"Progress!''

"Just kidding.''

"Besides, you should call Robert if you need to talk to him.'' Jenny didn't feel up to explaining that she had no influence with Robert.

"I haven't been able to reach him.''

"I suppose he's not answering his phone.'' Jenny knew how Robert felt about interviews. Apparently he also felt that way about having his picture in the paper with her. "But I don't know how to reach him, either.''

"You don't?'' Jenny's sister sounded surprised. "He made it sound like you two were friends.''

"Yeah, well—''

"He kissed you,'' her sister said emphatically. "With your hair net on. Even Mom thinks the man is serious about you.''

"That's just because she watched some program on television yesterday.''

Jenny heard the doorbell ring and the sound of her mother's footsteps as she started to walk toward the front door.

"Look, I've got to go,'' Jenny said into the phone. She didn't dare leave her mother alone with some reporter. "Someone's at the door. I'll call back in a few minutes.''

"No problem.''

Jenny clicked the phone off as she set it on the kitchen counter. She smoothed back her hair as she walked toward the door separating the kitchen from the living room. Knowing her mother, she would offer the reporter refreshments if Jenny didn't act fast.

Jenny called out to the reporter as she started to swing the door open. "I'm so sorry, but we can't—"

The day had started out gray and it was still gray. There wasn't much light coming into the living room and Jenny's mother had the lamp by the sofa lit. It created a warm, yellow glow in one corner of the room.

The reporter had already been invited into the living room and he stood with his back to the kitchen door Jenny was swinging open. For some reason, her mother was showing him the family pictures on the wall.

Even in the gray half-light of the room, Jenny still had to blink. The reporter's back showed off the plaidest plaid suit she had ever seen. Blue stripes met with shades of red and green. And the tip of the shirt that showed above the suit collar promised even more plaid.

"We aren't doing interv—" Jenny continued her speech until the reporter turned around.

She stopped midsentence. She stopped midstride. She was losing her mind.

"Robert?" She managed to croak out the name as she stood and stared.

"I told you I was coming," he said softly. "And you can call me Bob."

"Bob?"

Yes, she was definitely losing her mind.

"You told me Bobs wore plaid. I know it's a bit extreme. I thought you could use a laugh."

What she could use was a straitjacket.

"It's very clever." Jenny tried to pull herself together and smiled. "Really, very clever. Really."

Someday she'd laugh about it…maybe. Her sister would laugh soon enough, that's for sure.

"Bob's going to stay for some tea," Jenny's mother announced as though it was the most normal thing in the world. "I was just showing him the family pictures on our wall."

Jenny groaned inside. She knew what was coming.

"He thought your kindergarten picture was so cute," her mother boasted.

"That picture should be burned," Jenny said. Her hair had stood straight up. Big clumps of dark hair that no brush or curler could tame.

"Definitely cute." Robert smiled. His blue eyes crinkled just like Santa Claus's. Jenny swore to it. He looked harmless and congenial one minute and the next minute he turned into the playboy that he was. "You're still cute, for that matter."

"Thank you." Jenny smoothed down the linen dress she wore. "My hair does much better now."

"I don't know. I kind of like it when it's doing its own thing. It has a sense of freedom about it."

Jenny couldn't believe Robert—or Bob or whoever the man was—had come to her mother's door so they could discuss Jenny's hair. Of course not, she thought. He was a busy man. He must have another purpose. Ahhh, yes.

"You don't need to worry about any of my pictures appearing next to yours in any paper in the world," Jenny said as she walked over to the picture wall. "My mother would never let a reporter take one of these pictures off the wall. Would you, Mother?"

"Of course not." Jenny's mother sounded offended that the question was even asked.

Robert looked bewildered.

"I know you bought up all the pictures of us dancing in Dry Creek," Jenny explained. "I understand why you did it. I really do. But I don't think anyone will come here looking for another picture of me."

"You know about the pictures?" Robert sounded cautious.

Jenny nodded. "I know you were afraid a tabloid would pick one up and print it after Mr. Gossett...well, after he said those things—and so you bought the pictures from the kids."

"I bought the pictures the night they were taken."

Sometimes the earth turns slowly. Sometimes it spins like a top.

Jenny blinked. That couldn't be right. "But there weren't any reporters around that night."

"No," Robert quietly agreed.

"No one had said anything about us."

"No."

"Then why would you want the pictures?"

Robert glanced at her a little shyly. "Someday I thought we'd have a picture wall of our own."

Jenny's mother cleared her throat as she started toward the kitchen. "I think I'll go see about that tea now."

"But picture walls are for—" Jenny began.

"Families, I know. But I'm not pressuring you. I know we haven't known each other very long. I'm willing to wait."

Jenny tried to make sense of what she was hearing. "Wait for what?"

Robert smiled. "I'm just willing to wait, that's all. To let you adjust to the idea of me. I'm not the easiest person in the world to know."

Jenny didn't know what to say.

That didn't bother Robert. He continued. "I thought we'd start with a date. Maybe you'd go to a movie with me?"

Jenny could only nod.

Jenny couldn't understand it all. "Are you still

working to get off that list? Is that what you're do-ing?"

"Oh, it's too late for that. All I could do was to get them to knock me down to second place."

"So you're going to be one of the bachelors no matter what?" Jenny was trying to make sense of what she was hearing.

Robert nodded. "I could marry twins right now and it wouldn't bounce me off the list. I'm stuck with it."

If it wasn't the list, what was it? Jenny wondered. "So you're just trying out being Bob again—is that it?"

Robert shrugged. "Bob does sound friendly. But I can answer to either name. It's not a big deal."

"Of course it's a big deal," Jenny protested. "It's your name. I need to know what to call you."

"I was hoping you might call me dear—when you're comfortable with it, of course. But only when you're ready. The first step is a date."

Robert took a step closer. "And a kiss. That'd be a good place to start, too."

Jenny looked up as Robert bent down. They met and the world tilted just a little bit. The air grew warmer. The room grew darker.

"I hear bells," Robert murmured.

Jenny listened to the hissing and whispered, "Teakettle."

"No." Robert smiled softly. "I think it's bells. It'll always be bells with you and me."

Epilogue

Bob was right, Jenny thought six months later. The first step was the date. She'd fallen a little in love with him over buttered popcorn in the movie house. She'd fallen hopelessly in love the next day when he showed her the album he'd used to mount their kissing pictures.

Except for the one picture they sent to Jenny's sister, the other pictures from Dry Creek were all proudly mounted in the plastic sheets of Bob's family album—even the ones that were missing a head or two.

Jenny and Bob both went back to Dry Creek to continue cooking for the teenagers and to begin regular meetings with the pastor. They laughed together, they talked, and they built a pyramid of empty pudding cups for her sister's first assignment in her new job writing for a health magazine.

No one was surprised when Bob and Jenny set a wedding date of September 1.

The Dry Creek church polished the pews for the day even though no outside reporters were allowed. The Billings paper was allowed to run a small paragraph in their Newly Married section written by their local reporter. It primarily talked about the bride's gown.

Even though no outside reporters were allowed at the ceremony in the Dry Creek church, there was no lack of people taking pictures.

When the minister gave the signal for Bob to kiss his bride, fifty disposable cameras flashed almost in unison.

"Now I know why love is blind," Bob whispered to Jenny as he nuzzled her lip. "It's all the flashes."

"Kiss her again," one of the teenagers with a camera yelled. "I've got plenty—"

"What does he mean by that?" Jenny leaned into her husband.

"I got them special cameras—fifty shots apiece."

"That means—"

"That's right—they're set for fifty kisses tonight."

"Hmmm," Jenny said as her husband's lips met hers again. "Fifty's a nice number."

* * * * *

Dear Reader,

Thank you for coming with me once again to Dry Creek, Montana. I have enjoyed writing this book and hope you have enjoyed spending more time with the people who live in this fictional town.

In this book of the Dry Creek series, I'd ask you to especially think about the old man, Mr. Gossett. His bitterness toward others has been evident in all the books in the series, but in this book you discover that his bitterness goes back many years to a grudge against the town of Dry Creek and a disappointment with a woman who did not love him. The combination of all this pent-up unvoiced resentment soured the old man until he was willing to steal from his neighbors and even contemplate the murders of Jenny and Robert.

We all have disappointments. We have all been wronged by someone sometime. These experiences can sour us unless we talk about them, pray about them and practice forgiveness toward others. I like to meditate on these words in the Lord's Prayer—"forgive us our debts as we forgive the debts of others." It puts forgiveness in perspective for me.

Again, thank you for making the trip to Dry Creek with me.

Sincerely yours,

Janet Tronstad

Next Month From Steeple Hill's™

Love Inspired®

Loving Treasures
by
Gail Gaymer Martin

After her past heartache, Jemma Dupre wanted to
prove she could stand on her own. However,
Philip Somerville was nothing like her late husband.
Dependable and loving, he offered her everything she
had ever dreamed of. But could he show her that God's
plan included the treasure of a second chance at love?

**Don't miss
LOVING TREASURES**
On sale June 2002

Next Month From
Steeple Hill®'s

Love Inspired®

His Hometown Girl

by

Jillian Hart

Having narrowly escaped
a loveless marriage,
Karen McKaslin was
counting her blessings.
However, she never
dreamed Mr. Right was
waiting for her on the wrong
side of the tracks, praying
she'd see in his eyes what he
didn't dare say....

Don't miss
HIS HOMETOWN GIRL
On sale July 2002